the 13ᵀᴴ FLOOR

Graphics Design: Ace Collins
Colorized by Patty Allison
Model: Alison Johnson
Interior and Back Cover Design: Melinda Martin
Editor: Deb Haggerty
Published in Association with: Hartline Literary Agency

Library Cataloging Data
Names: Collins, Andrew (Ace) (Collins Andrew (Ace)) -
Title: The 13th Floor / Andrew (Ace) Collins
174 p. 23cm × 15cm (9in × 6 in.)
Description: Elk Lake Publishing digital eBook edition | Elk Lake Publishing Trade paperback edition | Massachusetts: Elk Lake Publishing, 2016.
Summary: Helen Meeker Lives!
Identifiers: ISBN-13: 978-1944430252 (trade) | 978-1944430245 (POD) |
978-1944430269 (ebk.)
1. Helen Meeker 2. FDR 3. Oil refineries 4. WWII 5. Explosives 6. Private investigators 7. Exposes

the 13ᵗʰ FLOOR

Ace Collins

 Elk Lake
Publishing, Inc.

Plymouth, Massachusetts

CHAPTER I

Wednesday, July 22, 1942
4:07 a.m.
Balch Refinery, Houston, Texas

The flames along the waterfront warehouse angrily pushed more than ninety feet toward the clear, star-filled Texas sky. The smell of gasoline mixed with the odor of burned rubber was causing some onlookers to become sick to their stomachs. And with each gust of supercharged wind, the immense heat generated by the burning fuel drove a beleaguered band of firefighters into a full-scale retreat. This was a battle the men were not going to win.

"Millions of dollars going up in flames," a tall, muscular FBI agent named Frank Laday muttered as he drove up to the scene in a light blue 1941 Ford Super Deluxe Coupe. After adjusting his hat and checking the knot in his blue tie, he switched off the flathead V-8 motor and reached for the door handle. Once outside the car, he stoically stood for a moment, as if paying tribute, his face reflecting the flames.

Stepping out into the humid air, Laday's partner, Jack Dollar, studied the scene and sadly nodded. Dollar, at five-eleven, was four inches shorter than his partner, but they shared the same black hair, clear blue eyes, and taste in suits. Dollar's off-the-rack model was dark blue and tonight was matched with a white shirt and striped tie.

While they clearly shopped at the same stores, under the clothes the men were cut from a much different cloth, which was clear from their reactions to this coastal disaster. Dollar's reaction wasn't about the money—that would be covered by insurance—what concerned him was the cost to the war effort. This burning fuel was badly needed on both fronts and was also a necessary element in running the machines of industry right here in the States. Each day a refinery was down meant more lost lives in Africa, Italy, and the Pacific as well as fewer products being manufactured to help guarantee an American victory.

"How many does this make?" Dollar asked as the two men moved forward and leaned against the front of their car's triple chrome grills.

"Four in the last month," Laday grumbled as he removed a package of Lifesavers from his pocket and popped one into his mouth. "You want one?" he asked offering the package to his partner.

"No, I'm fine," Dollar announced with a wave of his right hand.

"Let me see now," Laday began while holding his fingers up in the light. There was San Diego, Newark, and Mobile. They all went up about the same time of the night and in a similar fashion."

"And yet the fire experts found nothing to point to arson," Dollar added as she crossed his arms and frowned.

"Nope."

The pair remained mute as four more fire trucks rolled up to the scene in a futile effort to slow the blaze down. According to the gold badging on their doors, this quartet of vehicles had driven in from Texas City. The fresh crew, already dressed for action, leaped off the trucks and immediately went to work.

"Might as well just let it burn," Dollar added. "You can't fight a monster like this."

"We're pushing our people too hard," Laday noted as his eyes went from his partner and back to inferno. "That's what causing this mess. We're working the crews too many hours and they get careless. Exhaustion might not mean much in a shoe factory, but one person fading out in a place like this leads to disaster. And don't forget, we're using women in industrial jobs now. They're not made for this kind of labor or stress. That's why they're called the weaker sex. A woman gets tired, takes a break next to her station, goes to sleep, a cigarette in her hand and bang, the whole place goes up. You didn't see this kind of thing before women were placed in places they didn't belong. They should have left them at home or teaching school. Old Hoover's got it right. No women in the Bureau except the ones manning telephones or typewriters."

Dollar didn't debate his partner's opinion. After all, as a field agent, he knew what it was like to grind through long hours fueled by little more than coffee and grit. But his gut screamed there was more at work here than fatigue and what was playing out in front of them had nothing to do with women in the workforce.

"You seen enough?" Laday asked. "When the arson squad does their report, we can decide if this is a matter for the Bureau."

"You know as well as I do they'll find nothing, but my gut tells there's something funny going on here. I just know it!"

The frustration was easy to read in Dollar's voice. In his mind, negligence could be responsible for one or even two fires in a refinery, but not four in a month. Even if Hoover didn't buy it, this had to be an act of sabotage.

"You're wrong," Laday suggested as he moved back toward the driver's door. "It's likely just some doll who got careless—if there is anything more to it than that, then show me some proof."

"You know as well as I do there won't be any proof," Dollar barked. "There won't be anything left other than melted steel and ashes. Worse yet, twenty or more families will hold memorial services with nothing more than memories to bury. And the next day, they'll begin to clean up this lot and start rebuilding." His anger seething, the agent marched back to the car, slid in, and slammed the door.

"You need to keep this in perspective," Laday suggested as he eased into the Ford and hit the starter button bringing the V-8 almost silently to life. "These people knew the dangers when they went to work at this plant. They were paid well for their risks, and their families will get nice insurance checks to help them get over their loss. It's like being a coal miner; there are risks. The people who died in this mess played the odds, and they lost. The answer's not going to be finding some mysterious enemy setting off bombs to blow up refineries. No, this is only going to stop when we're smart enough to shorten the hours and give jobs like this to only men."

"And where do we find the men to fill all those jobs?" Dollar demanded. "The last time I looked, most of the able-bodied men were being drummed into the military."

"And who had a better chance of living through this day?" Laday shot back. "Those folks in the plant making the big bucks or the men on the front line getting paid peanuts? I'd rather be working with gasoline than dodging bullets. And let's not even talk about those who work in German refineries. They not only deal with the dangers of the plant operation but nightly visits by our bombers. So, it seems to me the people working in refineries in the US have it lucky."

"Tell that to their husbands, wives, or kids," Dollar suggested. "See what kind of response you get from them." He pointed out the windshield before adding, "Look over to the fence; you can see a bunch of them standing behind the chain link. Look at their faces. They deserve to know the real reason this happened."

"It was carelessness," Laday shot back. "You'll lose a lot less sleep if you accept that fact and move on. Besides, this isn't our gig. We're involved in finding the forces behind the black market. Focus on that assignment and quit trying to make too much out of some dame getting careless in place where she never belonged."

As the coupe rolled forward and the driver turned the Ford toward downtown, Dollar grimaced. He wouldn't be satisfied even after the report told him that no suspicious cause for the fire was found. There was a lot more going on here than met the eye and someone had to find out who was behind it and put them away.

THE 13TH FLOOR

CHAPTER 2

Wednesday, July 22, 1942
7:25 a.m.
Team Headquarters, Maryland

"Everyone ready to go?" Helen Meeker asked as she moved toward the back door of the large home serving as the team's center of operations.

"We're ready," Becca Bobbs assured her. "Gail's already out by the car and Clay is at the airstrip getting the DC-2 fueled. Next stop Mexico."

Meeker, itching for action, was dressed in black slacks and a matching shirt. On this occasion, she'd replaced her normal fedora with a Chicago Cubs baseball cap. After straightening the hat's bill and reaching for the doorknob to complete her exit, the phone rang. She glanced toward her partner and frowned.

"You better get it," Bobbs suggested. "Might be a change in plans."

Nodding, the team leader strolled back down the hall, ambled into the conference room and picked up the receiver. Taking a deep breath, she swept her dark, auburn hair back over her shoulder and announced, "What do you need?"

"Hey, Sis. I'm chirping from the big Eagle's lair and …"

"Does that mean you're in the Oval Office?" Meeker asked.

"Yeah, I am, and to put this in language your age group will understand, your cover's been blown."

"What do you mean?"

"Is the *Washington Sun* delivered to the estate each day?"

"Yeah, it and a dozen other newspapers," Meeker confirmed. "Why?"

"Well," Alison suggested, "you need to read it before you go anywhere or do anything. And that order comes from the top. Once your eyes roll through those words, call me back."

Meeker glanced across the table to a stack of newspapers. Setting the phone down, she strolled over to the dailies and sifted through five of them until she came across one she recognized as *The Sun*. Pushing the string off, she unrolled the paper and turned it to read the headline. Before the news of the war or the latest reports from Congress were six-inch-tall black capitals screaming, "**HELEN MEEKER'S ALIVE!**"

A suddenly shaky Meeker took a seat and began to quickly read the copy.

> Helen Meeker, who supposedly died in a late March plane crash, is actually very much alive and working with the President. Her death was faked so she could go undercover and deal with matters FDR wanted "off-the-books." Senator Andrew Mellon was flabbergasted when

he heard the news. He told this writer, "So now the President of the United States has become a king rather than an elected leader. Just like our enemy he has a band of secret black hats that do his bidding without rule of law or the oversight of Congress. I will be calling immediate hearings on this matter, and those behind it will be prosecuted to the fullest extent of the law. This is not democratic nor is it the way an American president should conduct the business of his office. If this issue is as dark as I fear, we might have to look into impeachment."

Mellon was not the only member of Congress who reacted to the news. Senator Jeb North saw the entire affair in a different light. "On the surface, I find this somewhat amusing. Here we are in the middle of a world war, and the President feels that a woman is needed to do major behind the scenes work in the field of intelligence. We all know that women cannot keep a secret; it is not in their nature. Besides, what could a woman offer to this country that would be of any great value other than working in an office, a home, or as a nurse? The mere fact we are starting to employ women in war production is simply absurd. I am sure that the rash of accidents we have recently witnessed in vital industrial plants will eventually be traced to females attempting to do jobs for which they are simply not suited."

The questions this newspaper and likely its readers want to know ... Where is Helen Meeker? What has she been doing over the last few months? Were her actions legal? J. Edgar Hoover has assured this newspaper he has men assigned to the task of bringing Meeker, who once worked with one of his agents, Henry Reese, on a famous kidnapping case, in for questioning. You can be assured *The Sun* will continue to cover this story in depth.

Meeker passed the paper to a curious Bobbs before walking back and picking up the phone. After dialing several numbers and going through the White House switchboard, she asked her sister, "What does the President want me to do?"

"You have little choice," came the quick reply, "you have to face the music. The team here has studied this for the last few hours, and there is no way to unwrite what has been written. You are once more alive, and we have to trot you out and show you to the American people. The good news, if there is any, is that everyone still believes Becca and Clay are dead. Thus, the team can go on to Mexico with Worel and pick up the package. If they need another body, you can send Dizzy Vance with them."

"At least, there's some good news," Meeker wryly cracked. "Do I just drive into town and pose for pictures? In other words, how do I make my grand entrance … my rebirth?"

"You need to go to Camp David," Alison suggested. "A team of advisors is there drawing up plans on how to best frame the reason for your faked death. We have already developed a few good scenarios that might satisfy the Congress and the American people. Right now, we just have to figure what we can release that you've done to make your service justified and weigh that against what to hold back to protect the remaining members of the team and our operation."

Meeker nodded, "I'll get my things together and make my way to Camp David. And Alison ..."

"Yes."

"Thanks for explaining this in a way I could understand."

"No problem, Sis. I'll save the slang for the next time we get together. I'll see you on the flip side of the platter."

The now exposed team leader put the receiver back in into the phone's cradle and glanced over to Bobbs. "I guess I don't have to tell you what that story means."

"Maybe you do," the woman suggested.

"Becca, you're in charge now, and you had better get started. It will be your call, but if I were you, I'd take Vance along. You'll need a team member to replace me to have all our bases covered."

"Are you all right?" a concerned Bobbs asked.

Meeker shook her head, "It's over. I guess the sham couldn't go on forever. I'll just have to get used to being back among the living."

"How did they find out?" Bobbs asked. "Who ratted you out?"

Meeker hadn't thought to ask that question. Glancing back at the phone she picked up the receiver and made a call to a secure number at the White House. It only took a few seconds for the President to pick up.

"Hello."

"It's Helen."

"As Winston would say, we have found ourselves in a sticky wicket."

"Yeah, so I see. And I'm sorry about that."

"It's not your fault, my dear. I was the one who created the team and faked your death."

"Thank you, sir, but somehow I must have slipped up. Someone must have spotted me. So here's the question. Do you know who gave *The Sun* the information?"

"As a matter of fact, we do, Helen. It was a former night-club singer named Lupino. Our sources tell us she sold the story for thirty thousand dollars to someone here in the Washington, and that person or organization fed it to the newspaper. After that, Miss Lupino dropped out of sight. In Alison's language, she vaporized."

"Yeah, I wondered what happened to her after Reggie Fister disappeared. Guess we know now."

"I'll see you at Camp David."

"Thanks," Meeker whispered. "Sorry I let you down."

After hanging up the phone Meeker looked toward Bobbs and solemnly announced, "Grace Lupino came out of hiding and sold her story."

"Why that little …"

Meeker cut her off. "At least, she didn't rat out you or the rest of the team."

"That doesn't mean she won't," Bobbs suggested.

She was right too. If Lupino was out there, she was in danger of revealing things that would expose the entire operation. So the nightclub songbird had to be found and moved to a secure location until after the war. Perhaps Meeker could, at least, accomplish that. But where would she start?

"While we're in Mexico," Bobbs asked, "what are you supposed to do?"

"I've been ordered to Camp David," she explained, "to work out a plan to make me look like some kind of a hero.

I'm betting the ultimate story will become I saved the country thanks to following the President's plans. Then, if there is no fallout, I will likely get to become a bond salesman or something."

"That's not you," the other woman observed, "leave that to the movie stars."

"Who knows what my future holds," Meeker said with a forced smile. "You have a job to do, and I need to get packed and out of here. Explain what has happened to the others and stay focused. I'm sure Alison will still be your contact when you get back. After all, there are still a lot of things we have to …" Meeker paused and frowned, "… I mean, you have to accomplish."

Bobbs sadly nodded, turned and hurried down the hall and out the back door.

After she watched her team drive out into the tree-lined path leading to the back entrance, Meeker deliberately walked over the radio and flipped it on. Thirty seconds later, the song, "Darn That Dream" by Benny Goodman and His Orchestra, filled the room. She frowned. Song scribe Eddie DeLange, who penned that hit, could have written those lyrics based upon Meeker's own life.

THE 13TH FLOOR

CHAPTER 3

Wednesday, July 22, 1942
10:35 a.m.
An alley in the central Washington, DC slum district

Tom Green, in his forties, had been with DC homicide for fifteen years. But, the divorced father of two kids had not grown used to seeing death. The faces of those whose murders he tried to solve haunted him. He constantly wondered about the victims' dreams, their unfinished business and the stories they never lived. On this unseasonably warm morning, as the tall, lanky cop studied the scene his men were processing, he tried to utilize logic over emotion and piece together what might have happened to a soul who had checked out of this world about forty years too soon. As Green circled the scene, he guessed, due to the way the body appeared, the small, dark-headed woman must have been murdered just before dawn. About that time, a bullet of unknown caliber had entered the back of her head and exited out the front. While the slug had not been found, there could be little doubt she had been killed instantly. Thus, she likely never had the chance to actually feel any pain or reach out and try to hold onto one last breath.

Pushing his hands into the pockets of his gray slacks, Green turned his light green eyes from the victim and looked down the length of the alley chosen to be the young woman's door to the next world. One glance assured him this was hardly a good place to die. In this grimy, rarely seen side of the nation's capital, in a part of town diplomats and elected officials didn't visit, people didn't as much live as simply survive. Happiness was an infrequent visitor here while pain and suffering never left.

The narrow brick pavement where the body rested was covered with mud and garbage. If you as much as touched one of the walls, you'd have to clean your fingernails. This was the underbelly of Washington, a place where a battle for life didn't start on December 7, 1941; this fight had been waged for generations.

A deeply scarred yellow cat, one of its ears nothing more than shredded skin, was digging through trash recently dumped out of a tenement apartment while another smaller feline was hopefully watching to see if there would be anything left when the big guy finished. The residents here were pretty much like those cats, a smaller one always waiting on the larger ones to throw them some scraps.

"Cap," a sixty-year-old, gray-headed man announced as he ambled away from the body.

"What do you know, Hank?" Green asked, grateful to be pulled from a reality that ate at his soul and challenged his belief in a loving God.

"She was dumped here," Wilson announced, "but there can be no doubt she was murdered somewhere else."

Green nodded and kicked the pavement with his foot. "I kind of figured that. It's obvious she wasn't dressed for a night out in this neighborhood. The last time an outfit that cost that much was in this part of town was when the President's wife decided to come for a visit to see how poor folks really lived."

Wilson shook his head. "This just seems sadder than most of our cases."

"Death's always sad, especially when it concerns a young woman." A chill ran down his spine as if the grim reaper had just passed by. After once more scanning the alley, Green continued his search for answers. "Now, any idea who she is?"

"We don't have a specific identification," the other cop explained, "but we have a few interesting items that might spell out why she was killed. It's either that or someone has a wicked sense of humor."

Green looked back to the body and grimly frowned. There was nothing funny about this ... nothing at all. Yet perhaps, if the sergeant was right, they might find something to help them narrow things down. Strolling back to the victim, the captain went to one knee to get a better view of the woman who had died much too soon. She had been pretty, in an exotic fashion. As he had earlier noted, she was dressed well, as if for an evening out on the town, and the lack of blood around the wound indicated she had been cleaned up before being dumped in the alley. Her open eyes were dark, her lips ruby red, rouge had been carefully applied to her cheeks, she was wearing eyeshadow and false eyelashes. She was dressed in a blue silk suit that looked as if tailored for her body. Her hands were covered with matching gloves. Her pumps were perhaps a shade darker. She must have been ready for a night out on the town, but instead, she had a date with death.

"She was beautiful," Wilson noted.

"Was is the operative word," Green observed. "She's too well-dressed to be a hooker."

"That's what I thought," the older man chimed in.

As he continued to study the woman, the captain asked, "You hinted that you had something that might help us ID her?"

"It's kind of strange," Wilson explained. "There was no billfold or driver's license in her purse, but there was some money, a package of cigarettes, a matchbook …"

Green rose and cut the man off. "You said you found a matchbook?"

"Yeah."

"Where from?"

"The Grove. I think it's a nightclub."

"I know the place well," Green noted. "It's where a lot of society plays. As I remember, it is one of the clubs Dick Diamond owns. So I guess we can start with him. Have the crew get a picture of her face and print me a copy. I'll take it with me when I make an official visit to The Grove." After standing and once more pushing his hands deep into his pockets, the homicide captain asked, "What else did you say she had in her bag?"

"The purse must have weighed a ton," came the reply.

"Why?"

"Because she was carrying thirty silver dollars."

"What about her other cash."

"There was none," Wilson explained, "just thirty silver dollars."

Why would any woman in Washington be carrying around that much silver? Green chewed on that mystery before looking back to his partner. "You said she had some cigarettes too."

"Yeah, Lucky Strike Red." Wilson looked back at his notes and then added, "We got one other thing that's pretty weird too."

"It should go well with everything else then," the captain cracked. "This is one bizarre case. I kind of feel like should call in Philo Vance."

Wilson cocked his head to the side. "Is he real? I thought he was just a movie character."

Green shook his head. "Forget it, you said you had something else."

"Yea, it's a page torn out of a Bible. Look at what's underlined."

Green took the single sheet and glanced at the top. It was from the twenty-seventh chapter of Matthew.

> *Then Judas, which had betrayed him, when he saw that he was condemned, repented himself, and brought again the thirty pieces of silver to the chief priests and elders, saying, I have sinned in that I have betrayed the innocent blood. And they said, What is that to us? See thou to that. And he cast down the pieces of silver in the temple, and departed, and went and hanged himself.*

"It appears she sold someone out," the captain noted, "and that person knew something about the Bible." He glanced back to his assistant. "I wish Philo Vance really was the real deal now, I could use him. This reads just like a radio detective script. Or maybe, because of the torn page from the Bible, I should call Billy Sunday in as a consultant."

"Huh?"

Green looked back to the sergeant and shrugged. "Never mind, Hank. You oversee the operation here; I'm going to get back to headquarters and check our missing persons reports. Maybe she's in those files. When you all get me a picture printed, I'll go over and see Mr. Diamond."

As Green strolled through the trash back toward the end of the alley, he once again paused to observe the cats. The bigger one was allowing the calico to share the morning meal. Just proved that if you waited long enough, charity would visit even the poorest of neighborhoods. Turning his eyes from the felines to the wall, the captain spotted a faded promotion poster. There were three more just like it within a dozen feet, and none of them were likely ever seen by anyone other than garage men, rats, or alley cats. He figured the person who posted these bills must have been paid by the sheet.

Stepping closer, Green read the words on the faded advertisement. *Hear the melodic strains of the dynamic Grace Lupino at The Grove.* He was about to move on when he noted the star's publicity picture. There was something about that photo.

Grabbing a corner of the poster, the captain tore it from the wall and marched back down to the crime scene. Holding it beside victim, he grimly smiled.

"What you got, Cap?" Wilson asked.

"The identity of this woman," came the crisp reply. "She was a nightclub singer named Grace Lupino."

"Yeah," Wilson said as he snapped his fingers. "I remember her; she disappeared a while back. At the time she went missing, she was a hot local act too. What are the odds of you finding her poster in the very alley where she was dumped?"

"Too long," the captain assured him. "Look at the back of this one. The paste is fresh. There are a few more up toward the street. Someone left these here to make our job a bit easier."

"Why? That doesn't make any sense."

"Because of a story in *The Washington Sun,* this dame is hot. My guess is they're trying to frame Mr. Diamond. Do me a favor, Hank, and keep a lid on her identity. Don't tell anyone else who she is. Let's keep her a Jane Doe until I pin down who nailed her. And I'll bet it wasn't Mr. Diamond."

THE 13TH FLOOR

CHAPTER 4

Wednesday, July 22, 1942
6:45 p.m.
Camp David, Maryland

Still dressed casually in black, Meeker observed the President and his press secretary reviewing the actions of her team. As they whispered to each other in the corner of the retreat's private study, she sat on the other side of the room listening to the radio news. Not surprisingly, her story was the main attraction. It seemed the search for Helen Meeker had pushed everything else into the shadows.

"Helen," the President called from his chair.

As she strolled over to join the Commander in Chief, the press secretary exited. Taking the seat the man had just vacated, Meeker watched FDR place a cigarette into his long holder, slip the holder into his mouth, strike a match and light up. After taking a long drag, he exhaled and frowned.

"This Lupino woman has created quite a mess for us," he flatly announced as the cigarette's smoke hovered just above his head. "At the very least, she has taken my most important operative out of the field."

"She has the information to do much, much more," Meeker suggested.

"Yes, she does," he agreed. "Or rather she did."

"Did?" the woman was confused. Why the change in tense?

After another puff on his cigarette, the President announced, "The police found her body in an alley this morning. She'd been shot execution style. In her purse was a reference to Judas and thirty pieces of silver."

"What?" the woman whispered. "The press will no doubt tie this to me and then you. They'll say we did her in. I can just imagine what Senator Melon will make out of this."

"Actually," the President suggested, "they won't do either. The press doesn't have the story and, for the time being, they are not going to get it. The man in charge of the investigation is an old friend of mine. Tom fully understands the delicate nature of this news and, as there was no identification found with the body, he has listed the victim as unknown. Since Grace Lupino has no next of kin, I don't think anyone is going to be too interested in coming to the morgue to look at the body. The newshounds will see this as the murder of a woman of the evening. Thus, it will never make it off a back page."

"Describing her that way is not much of a stretch," Meeker noted. "But who would have her murdered and then set her up as a Judas? This got nasty really fast!"

"Whoever set this up wanted you to look bad and that dirt to rub off on me." The President took another draw on his smoke, seemingly enjoying the taste as it lingered in his mouth and lungs before asking, "Do you have anyone in mind."

"Fister?" Meeker suggested.

"I thought he was dead."

"We all did," she announced, "but I'm now wondering if the man who died in the private sanitarium was his twin. When Reggie disappeared, we assumed he had disappeared with Lupino, but what if he went to the hospital to finish off his brother and, in the process, the two switched places. Alistar might well have overpowered Reggie. It also makes sense for Alistar to have been the one gunning for Teresa Bryant in Illinois. Reggie just wasn't the type to have been a triggerman."

"Then we need to find Fister," the President suggested.

"And the man who gives him his orders."

"I have another source who echoes what you suggest on the mystery man, but for the time being, you can't go after him or anyone else. For the time being, we need to remake your image."

"And how do you suggest that?"

"Well," he announced as he leaned back in his wheel-chair, "I can't give you credit for getting the gold back to Fort Knox as that bit of intrigue was never released to the press. The kidnappings are off-limits as well. And the media would fry us if we admitted you went behind the lines in Germany. Besides, that would put our underground friends in danger. So we're limited to one thing."

"What's that?" Meeker asked. "It seems you pretty much just burned through all our team's accomplishments."

The President's smile was so large it pushed his glasses up higher on his nose. After setting his cigarette in the ashtray, he explained. "We will finally give you credit for saving Winston's and my lives. There is a script you need to study that frames this whole affair in such a way we will come out smelling like a rose. It also clearly spells out why I was forced to fake your death. Tomorrow, you will hold a press conference where you will use your brains and charm to fully explain what we were doing."

"There are a couple senators who won't let it go at that," she suggested.

"And neither will Hoover," the President cracked. "But I have my ways with him. On Senator Melon, let him call his committee meeting. Let him grill you until he is blue in the face. I have no doubt you can answer every question in such a way as to take the heat off me and make him looked like the power grabbing, blubber butt he is."

"In the meantime, he will frame you as a dictator and a menace to America."

Roosevelt nodded. "He wants to run against me in two years. This is the way he'll position himself as the other party's frontrunner. It will be your job to find a way to have him rethink that."

"You're expecting a lot."

"Always have," he shot back, "and now I'm going to my room and catch up on the war reports. You study that script and learn what you need to know. The press conference will be at ten tomorrow morning in the White House. Be ready to be turned on the spit a few times. You also might be prepared for your role as a media star. You're about to be very famous. Who knows, our men in uniform might be using your picture as their pinup rather than Betty Grable."

"I hope not," Meeker sighed.

CHAPTER 5

Wednesday, July 22, 1942
7:02 p.m.
Ambassador Hotel Dining Room, Washington, DC

Teresa Bryant, dressed in a gray dress, a matching jacket, and purple blouse, strolled in, stopped and casually surveyed the upscale dining room. The drone of a hundred different conversations blended with the strains of a five-piece band playing the latest in swing music. The male clientele sitting at the linen-draped tables were dressed in either suits or military dress uniforms. The women were outfitted like Hollywood starlets or grand dames of society. Cigar smoke hovered in the air mixed with the scents of seafood and booze. In a time of public conservation, this was an exercise in excess.

Toward a far window, an elegantly dressed older woman sat alone sipping on what appeared to be a glass of red wine. After studying her hostess' blue dress and diamond-draped wrists, Bryant slipped across the room to the small, out-of-the-way table.

"Mrs. Root?"

The woman looked up and smiled, "My friends call me Gertie. You are no doubt Miss Teresa Bryant. And what do your friends call you?"

Not missing a beat, Bryant cracked, "I really don't have any friends, but you can call me Teresa."

"Have a seat, Teresa. This meal is on my tab, so if you find something you want, feel free to order it. By the way, the lobster is amazing!"

Bryant eased into a chair and scanned the menu. As the waiter approached, the guest looked back to her benefactor and suggested, "You have been here many times; why don't you order for me."

"Would you like a glass of wine?"

"No," Bryant quickly replied, "I'll take iced tea."

Root nodded, looked back at the red-coated waiter and pointed to the menu. "We will both have the lobster with corn and boiled potatoes. I believe you heard the woman's drink order."

"Yes, ma'am."

After the man strolled back toward the kitchen, Bryant looked into Root's round face. "I'll admit to being surprised that you called me today. I had no idea you even knew who I was."

"I saw you one day at the Capitol Dining Room," the woman explained. After taking a sip of wine, she added, "A friend knew you worked at the FBI. So I called J. Edgar's office and went from there."

"Why the interest in me? I don't have connections, money or a prominent name. I'm not old Washington, and I'm not a member of the DAR. To put it mildly, I'm a nobody, and you are obviously a member of society. So not only do we not play on the same team, we are not even in the same league."

"To be frank, my dear," Root smugly answered, "I have very little interest in you. Do you know who my husband is?"

Impressed with the woman's frankness, Bryant chimed in, "General Jefferson Root."

"Because of my spouse," Root noted, "we are forced to give many parties at our home. Those affairs are much more interesting if there are beautiful, young women serving as … how shall I put this … decorations."

The term made the hair on the back Bryant's neck stand up, but she didn't allow her disgust to show. Besides, having the opportunity to mix and mingle with the Washington movers and shakers would suit her just fine. She was in the information game, and there was no better place to find it than where the booze freely flowed. Still, she didn't want to appear too eager.

"There are always interesting people to visit with at parties," Bryant replied. "Especially during times of war, but I doubt if I'd know what to say."

"The question becomes are you interested?"

"I might be," Bryant answered. "What's required?"

"I would expect you to dress in such a way as to show off your considerable charms." Root allowed her eyes to fall from her guest's face to her body.

The woman was now pushing the envelope. What was she really after? Was she looking for a hostess or something more?

"I have my limits," Bryant noted.

"I'm sure you do," Root replied. "I'm not suggesting you be anything more than a piece of art. This would be a 'look but don't touch' arrangement. And, if you agree to be that piece of art, I will allow you to shop at the finest stores in town and buy a few things that go with that wonderful, exotically dark complexion. I will pay for everything."

"What are you really after?" Bryant demanded.

"Teresa, let me be frank. My husband needs votes in Congress as well as the support of other leaders in the military … both ours and our allies. You will charm those people. As you get to know them, and they become free around you, I will tell you what you need to say, and you will say it."

"I tend to speak my own mind."

"Sweetheart, so do I." Root raised her eyebrows, "And in your position, you will learn to speak *my* mind. Do you understand? My mind, not yours, is what matters."

"I get where you're headed, Mrs. Root."

"Good. Now I've chatted with Hoover, and he wants you to do this just as much as I do. Your charms can work for both my husband and the FBI. Do I need to say more?"

Root was extremely confident in her pitch. She seemed sure she would not be turned down. Yet, she had underestimated her foe this time. Bryant couldn't be bought off with shopping sprees or by rubbing elbows with the top brass. She had her own agenda. Still, for the moment playing along might just give her a bit more of what she really needed. There were people at those parties she could pump for information and having that access would allow her to cut even deeper into Washington power base. So this wouldn't be Root playing her, she would be playing Root.

"Is it a deal?" Root asked.

"Let's take it one party at a time," Bryant responded cautiously.

"One party a time it will be," Root agreed.

Neither spoke as the food was brought to their table. Only after the waiter departed did the older woman pose her next question. "What's your ethnic background?"

Bryant didn't immediately answer. Instead, she cut into her lobster, dipped a piece in butter and brought it to her mouth. It was every bit as good as advertised. Finally, after letting the inquiry hang for a while, she looked back to her host, smiled and asked, "Does it matter?"

"For your role at my house," Root assured her, "it does not. But you are so exotic-looking, I simply wanted to know where you came from."

"My people are Caddo."

"Caddo?" Her tone showed she didn't recognize the term.

"American Indian."

"Oh, that explains those exquisite cheekbones. I wish white people had that trait."

"Your people have something much better," Bryant quickly suggested.

"What's that?"

"Power."

"I suppose we do," Root noted. "Now, after we eat, I'll tell you about a party you need to attend tomorrow night at our house. Oh, and don't worry, J. Edgar will allow you time off to shop for just the right outfit. I would suggest something that hugs your hips and dips down at the neck. I think you would look perfect in royal blue too."

THE 13TH FLOOR

CHAPTER 6

Thursday, July 23, 1942
9:07 a.m.
The pressroom at the White House, Washington, DC

Meeker had chosen a conservative navy suit and white blouse for her public rebirth. As she waited in the hall to be introduced, she was almost sick. Everything she had worked so hard to created was about to disappear. No longer would she be fighting the war on her own terms, dealing with larger than life issues and spending her days and nights on the edge between life and death. By acknowledging she was alive, she would lose her ability to do what she loved ... the very things that allowed her to escape the rules and thinking that had confined women for centuries. So in a very real sense, coming back to life would be a great deal like dying.

An aid signaled for her to step forward. Taking a deep breath, she slowly walked out to the lectern. As she stood in front of the anxious crowd of reporters, flashbulbs popped from every corner of the room. On this occasion, the male members of the media would have likely not even noticed Carole Landis if she had walked out in a bathing suit and heels. The only thing on anyone's mind was the sordid story of Helen Meeker. At least, that is the way the story had been painted in the morning papers. The question yet to be answered: "Could this press conference turn the tables and recast her into the role of both victim and hero?"

A lottery had been conducted as to who got the first question, and the winner was veteran reporter Jake Scott of *The Post*. The distinguished New York-born scribe had been a part of the capital landscape for decades. Sadly, for a man who was so bright, his question showed no imagination.

"Miss Meeker, exactly where have you been, and what have you being doing the last five months?"

Helen took a deep breath and then followed the script constructed by the President's staff. With all eyes fixed on her, she explained, "At the President's suggestion, I have been in hiding. I was involved in stopping an attempt on the President's life in a secret meeting in upstate New York, and when the assassin escaped from FBI custody, Mr. Roosevelt thought it would be best if I were to disappear."

"Why was that?" another reporter barked from the back of the room.

Assistant press secretary Richard Wentworth stepped to the microphone to explain. "Miss Meeker did not want to disappear. In fact, she argued against it. Simply put, she was responsible for saving the lives of both the President and Winston Churchill, and the man responsible for the attack vowed to seek revenge on Miss Meeker. After his escape, he did manage to shoot Helen, and it took a major operation to save her life. At that point, we felt we needed to find a way to hide her away until the fugitive was caught or killed. When the unfortunate plane crash took the lives of Becca Bobbs, Henry Reese, and Clay Barnes, we felt we had the perfect ruse to employ for taking Miss Meeker out of the public's eye and off the murderer's radar, so we used it."

"So your death was faked?" Milt Freeman of the *New York Press* asked.

Meeker stepped back to the microphone, "Yes, it was. I would rather not have done this, but I was told protecting me was draining the government of valuable manpower. So by having my attacker think I was dead, my bodyguards could go back to vital work concerning the war effort."

Another reporter quickly shouted out, "Why weren't we told about the attempt on Mr. Roosevelt's life?"

"The President believed," Meeker immediately explained, staying on script, "that because the meeting between he and Mr. Churchill was secret, it would be in the best interest of both countries to keep it out of the press. If this had happened at any time other than during a state of war, it would have been immediately released."

"What did you do to save the President's life?" Freeman hollered. "Give us the details."

"I acted on a tip and disarmed the British agent who was working for Germany before he could fire. It wasn't that big a deal. I would like to tell you more but doing so would reveal certain classified information that must remain secret at this time."

Wentworth stepped forward offering information to polish Meeker's role as a hero. "I have a press release that fully explains what role Miss Meeker played as well as quotes from both Mr. Roosevelt and Mr. Churchill. I will be handing that out at the end of the press conference. Are there any more questions concerning Miss Meeker's time when she was thought to be dead?"

"I have one," a well-dressed, sixty-year-old man cried out from the second row. "I'm Bill Taylor with the *Los Angeles Times*."

"What is your question, Mr. Taylor?" Meeker asked. "And before you ask it, might I add how much I enjoyed your stories from the war front in the Pacific."

"Thank you for those words," he began, seemingly flattered by the woman's observation. "Now, Miss Meeker, I want to know if there is any truth to the story you were actually working uncover on covert projects that the President assigned? And is it true that those projects did not have the approval of Congress, the intelligence community or the military?"

"Mr. Taylor," Meeker announced with a coy smile, "do I look like a spy or a gun-toting field agent?"

"You didn't answer my question," the reporter pointed out.

"No, I didn't," she admitted. "And I wish I could tell you I've been involved in doing the work of this country here and even behind the lines in Germany. I wish I could tell you I have saved lives, thwarted enemy actions, and uncovered international secrets. I wish I could brag about being a real life Wonder Woman, but the fact is I'm a woman who couldn't even measure up to securing a minor position with the FBI. J. Edgar Hoover deemed me unworthy. So why would the President of the United States trust me to run a covert intelligence operation? It seems all I can put on my résumé is stumbling into a plot and being lucky enough to get between an assassin and the leaders of the free world."

A disappointed press corps murmured among themselves for a few seconds before Taylor asked another question. "If what you say in true, where is the assassin today?"

"We don't know," Meeker admitted. "The British did not want his name released when the event happened for fear of it dropping morale back in the UK. You see, the assassin was a British military hero. This morning, Mr. Churchill gave us permission to release the man's name and photograph so that the press, the public, and all law enforcement agencies can help us find and punish him."

"That's correct," Wentworth added as he stepped again to the podium. "There is a packet for each of you that gives complete information on the man. The name he was using as member of the British armed forces was Reggie Fister. Many of you might have covered his days as a celebrity here in Washington. Since that time, we have discovered Reggie was actually his twin brother, and this Fister had assumed his identity. The name of the man who tried to kill both Roosevelt and Churchill is actually Alistar Fister. You may consider him Public Enemy #1. There is a reward of one hundred thousand dollars for him dead or alive."

Wentworth glanced toward Meeker and nodded. He then turned back to the press. "I think you know the real story now. So why don't you pick up your packets and get America involved in tracking down this dangerous undercover Nazi agent."

As the press dove for the materials, Meeker strolled out the door, down the hall and onto a porch. Relieved the media now had a different rabbit to chase, she leaned against the wall and studied the White House's landscaped grounds.

"Did you know one president actually grazed livestock on the grass in this yard?"

Meeker looked to her right and directly into the brown eyes of Senator Andrew Melon. The man looked like a turkey vulture in human guise. A wide, almost evil smile spread from check to check as it forced his three chins over his shirt collar.

"I understand President Wilson kept sheep," she cracked, displaying her knowledge of history.

"You've done your homework," he laughed. "I was a young man back then. I actually walked on the grass and quickly discovered, because of the animals, I had to be careful where I stepped. What you told the press today equals the same thing those sheep left on that yard."

"Believe what you want," Meeker suggested. "As one of your colleagues noted, I'm just a girl. I couldn't be worth much to the President or anyone else."

"Jeb North is a fool," Melon spat, "but I'm not. You were by the far the most capable person in that room today. I also think you're the most dangerous, and I'm still going to call you to testify before my committee. On that stage, you will have to swear to tell the truth and, if you don't, then you will be spending some time behind bars."

She glared at the senator. "I'm guessing this is the not the same kind of bar you visit each night."

Ignoring her quip, he pushed harder and deeper with his threats. "For more than a seven years, I've been looking for a way to end this country's worship of Franklin Roosevelt. I almost had him when he tried to pack the Supreme Court, but he survived that misstep. This time, thanks to you, I have him. The confidence of the American people in this leader will fall to nothing when I get you up on the Hill."

"And then you'll get to redecorate the White House to suit your taste?" she asked.

He grinned and reached into his coat pocket. After removing a folded piece of paper, he whispered, "This is an engraved invitation to meet before the intelligence committee on Monday morning. Nothing short of death," he paused and laughed, "a real death this time, can keep you from being there. I can't wait to strip you bare. It will be a lovely sight."

Meeker watched the big man turn and happily amble down the porch toward the parking lot. Though she hadn't shown it, he had shaken her. If somehow he had questioned Grace Lupino before she died, he likely knew a great deal. To protect the President and herself she had to find out what Melon had learned before she testified.

THE 13TH FLOOR

CHAPTER 7

Thursday, July 23, 1942
1:05 p.m.
Progreso, Mexico

After a night of rest on the stretch of deserted beach, and a morning watching locals paddle small boats out to inspect the floating debris left by the sinking U-boat, Henry Reese and Fritz Klein began their trek to the small fishing village of Progreso. Even with a breeze coming off the Gulf, the heat and humidity were stifling. As they trudged through the soft sand, the pair quickly broke out in a full sweat.

"Kind of different from Germany," Reese noted.

"Have you ever visited my country?" Klein asked.

"Mostly under the cover of darkness," the American explained. "I've also seen it from the air. Wonder how much of your Fatherland will be left when the war is over. The way our bombers hit your cities, I'm guessing not much."

The German sadly nodded. "Not something I like to think about. Where in America are you from?"

"A lot of places," Reese answered as he continued to move down the beach. "My dad kind of wandered from job to job and place to place. He must have been part gypsy."

"So do you miss any place in particular?"

"I miss them all," Reese assured his uninvited guest. "A part of me longs to see the wheat fields of Kansas, and another wants to climb mountains in Colorado. In truth, if we didn't have to meet someone, I wouldn't mind spending a few hours right here on this beach. I'd kind of like to be anywhere people weren't killing each other and wrapping those deaths in a flag of patriotism."

"Talk like that," Klein warned, "would get you killed where I'm from."

Reese nodded. Talk like that wouldn't make him any friends back home either. But he was sick of death and the empty feeling killing left in his gut, and he didn't mind admitting it.

"How's your Spanish?" Klein asked the American as the first signs of the small city came into view.

Happy to have his mind pulled from memories of war, Reese shrugged. "I can communicate."

"And do we have a plan?" the German inquired.

Reese stopped, eyed-up his companion and smiled. "The plan depends upon you. Can you be trusted?"

"Be trusted to do what?"

The American nodded. "I can play the game as well as you, and we could dance around the obvious for days trying to out-clever each other, but I want things spelled out right now. Are we going into this town as comrades anxious to unite with my friends and go back to the States, or are we going in as enemies where you will make a break for it the first moment you get the chance?"

"You pull no punches," Klein noted.

"There is no time for them."

"Henry, you have the treasure you demanded, and I can see you have two guns. You even made the radio call to set up the meeting. So if I make a break, I'll just end up in a place where I don't know the language or customs and, on top of that, the locals likely don't view Germans in a favorable light. Now, if I had a pocket full of pesos, that last fact likely wouldn't matter. I could simply bribe my way to a place where I could get a ride back home. But I don't have any power. So as a man without weapons or means, who is wearing a U-boat commander's uniform, I'm don't like the percentages in trying to escape." The big man paused and grinned. "But, how do you see me? Am I going to a prisoner of war camp to spend the rest of my days, or do I have another option?"

Reese noted two fishermen pushing off from a dock about a hundred yards west. As their gaze met his, the locals waved. The American casually nodded and waved back. Only after the pair was well out in the water did he turn his eyes back to the German.

"I will do my best to keep you out of a POW camp, but that can only be accomplished if you can fully explain your loyalties."

"My loyalties?"

"Yes, are you still a Nazi or ..."

"I'm a German," Klein cut in. "That's what I will likely always be. But I'm a man who also has learned too much about his country to support what it is doing to ..." He paused, rubbed his hand over his face and frowned. "They killed my mother and who knows how many others. Even as we stand here, people are being slaughtered just because of their ethnic background."

"I know that," Reese assured him, "but all those words don't answer my question. Where do your loyalties lie?"

"At this point," Klein sadly noted, "they are at the bottom of the Gulf. I was loyal to my men, and they were loyal to me." He glanced out to the water. "I should be there with them."

"You're not."

The German turned his eyes back to the American. "I would have been if you hadn't stepped in. By the way, you're the man with all the treasure, where are your loyalties?"

"Ah," Reese answered, "the treasure. While you were sleeping this morning, I buried it. When the time comes, I'll dig it up and give it our government. They can figure out who really deserves it."

Klein ran his hand through his hair and shrugged, "And I'm supposed to believe you?"

"It's true."

"Henry?"

"How do you feel about religion?"

"I'm a Christian, and maybe the war has tossed a few more doubts my way, but I still believe most of what I've heard in church."

"I was raised a Lutheran," the German answered. "I never thought much about it until I found out about the camps. If I have to make a pledge of loyalty between those who claim Christ or those who built the death camps, then my choice is pretty clear. My loyalty to Hitler ended when I learned what the Nazis are hiding from the world."

Reese smiled. He had his answer. "Fritz, here's the plan. As you are wearing the German uniform, and the locals know about the sinking of that submarine, I'm taking you into town as my prisoner. My radio communication instructed me to find lodging at a central hotel under the name of Carl Jenkins. The people who will take us back to Washington will simply check at each hotel until they find someone registered under that name."

"Does that mean you will hold a gun on me?" Klein asked.

"In public," came the quick reply. "So let's get moving."

With the German leading the way, the pair walked into the outskirts of the small Mexican community. Over dirt streets, they made their way toward the heart of the sleepy city. About the time they spotted the town square, two men in suits stepped out of a cantina.

"What do we have here?" one asked in broken Spanish.

Neither looked Mexican. One was tall, blue-eyed and blond. The shorter one had dark hair and deep green eyes. Their pale skin indicated they hadn't spent much time in the sun. Reese was contemplating a way to reply to their question when he felt something cold in the middle of his back. He didn't have be told what it was.

"You have someone we want," a voice announced in German. "Let's move off the street and join my friends in the bar."

Seeing no reason to argue, Reese made a left turn and strolled into the poorly lit cantina. Not surprisingly, it was void of life.

"We've rented the place out for the day," the tallest man explained. "Set the gun on the first table to your right and then pull the other one out of your belt and do the same."

45

Reese complied.

"Now you can go over to the bar, turn around and face us."

It was twelve steps to the bar. As the American quickly crossed that distance, the man who had held the gun to his back closed and locked the cantina's door. Reese grimly grinned. It looked as though he had been booked for entertainment and would then be stuck with the bill.

CHAPTER 8

Thursday, July 23, 1942
2:15 p.m.
Jose's Cantina, Progreso, Mexico

The cantina was dark and smelled of cheap booze. Only two unshaded overhead one-hundred-watt bulbs illuminated the building's single large room. Behind the twenty-foot long bar was a counter holding, at least, fifty large bottles of liquor. In front were a dozen round, well-used round wooden tables scratched and stained from decades of service. The trio who had captured Reese stood, guns drawn, about ten feet in front of their prisoner. A now free Fitz Klein had opted to sit at the table where the American had dropped his guns.

"So you are the British agent?"

The man who posed the question was the blond whom Reese had first spotted in the doorway. He was likely in his mid-thirties, had a long scar on his left cheek, a nose that must have been broken a dozen times and eyes that indicated he'd spent a few evenings taking advantage of the local nightlife. He was not only big; he was ugly.

Reese answered the question with one of his own, "What makes you think that?"

"Because, my friend, we are the SS. While you were taking your trip across the Atlantic, we were here planning a welcoming party. As the Americans and their planes kept Herr Klein from sending back the information we needed on the underground leader, we will get it from you now. I believe that was a part of the agreed-upon bargain."

"And then what?" Reese demanded.

"Where is the treasure?" the German asked Klein.

"He buried it at the beach. I can lead you back there. It shouldn't be hard to find."

"Thank you, commander. And I'm sorry about your crew."

Klein coldly shrugged, "They died fighting for the Fatherland." He then looked back at Reese and added, "He's not going to give you the information. He never intended to. He's not even British. He's an American impostor."

The trio's leader nodded. "But does he know the answer?"

"I'm sure he does."

Turning his gaze back to Reese, the man in charge shrugged. "Do you want to make this easy, or do we do it the hard way?"

"I've never been easy," came the quick response.

The questioner dropped down into a chair while his companions set their guns on the table and removed their coats. In shirtsleeves, they looked like Popeye after he had consumed his spinach.

As Reese waited for the beating, he glanced over to Klein in disgust. The commander was now grinning like a cat. So much for all the noble talk, the German had just been setting him up for the kill. Suddenly, the memories of the Nazis he had killed were not nearly as painful. In fact, at this moment, he wished he had slaughtered a few more when working with the underground.

"Anything you want to say before my men give you your physical examination?" the man in charge asked.

Reese turned back to the German and grinned. "Yeah, I wish I'd never saved a drowning man. It was the worst mistake I ever made in my life."

If the American had hurt Klein's feelings, it didn't show. The sub commander tossed off the verbal assault with a shrug, smiled and waited for the men to start their jobs. Judging by their expressions, they enjoyed their work. The shorter of the two grabbed Reese's shoulders, spun him around, pulled his hands behind his back and then turned him to face the other shirt-clad German. A second later, an uppercut caught the American in the gut. The blow was so deep and powerful, Reese was surprised the man's fist didn't break his spine.

Looking up, Reese noted the German preparing a follow-up. Taking a deep breath, the American suggested, "Maybe you should have fought Joe Lewis instead of Max Schmeling."

"Max is my cousin," came the quick reply.

"I'm not doubting that."

Just as Reese readied his gut to take another blow, he detected a hint of movement on his left. A second later, a single shot rang out, and everyone froze. Looking beyond Max's hard-hitting cousin, the America watched the

SS team's leader waver in his chair before falling face first on the table. As the man's final breath escaped his lips, Reese felt the grip loosen on his arms. Pushing away from the two enforcers, the American turned toward Klein. Still sitting at the table, the commander's expression was grim and, in his hands, he held both of the guns Reese had earlier put down.

As the confused SS men looked on, Reese frowned. "Did you report to Germany that I survived the American's attack on my U-boat?"

Max's cousin shook his head. "Until we saw you walking up with the British spy, we didn't know you had lived through it."

"Just to remind you," Klein explained, "I told you he was an American. Anyway, glad you didn't put the word out I'm still breathing. I kind of like being dead. It works out far better for me." Standing, the man who now held all the power solemnly shook his head. "But, my friends, it doesn't work out so well for you. How many men have you killed?"

"Scores," the tall man answered as the other nodded in agreement.

"Well," the commander cracked, "then that makes this easier."

Two shots rang out from each gun. The shorter German immediately fell to the ground. Max's cousin wavered for a moment, his hands clutching his gut, before falling to his knees. He held that position for at least ten seconds and then pitched forward.

As the smoke cleared, Klein walked over to the front door, unlocked and opened it. He studied the street for a few seconds before stepping out leaving Reese alone with the three dead Germans.

Shaken, still feeling the pain from the blow he had received, Reese slowly moved over to a chair and eased down. He was not feeling in top form, but he was alive. A deep, painful breath filled his lungs with stale air still filled with the lingering smell of cordite. And as Reese's mind cleared, he began to evaluate the situation. Holsclaw's cover had not been blown, the American was close to home, members of the team were on their way to get him, and he had the treasure. For the last fact alone, the Brits would be pleased. Then like a bolt out of the blue, it hit him. Klein was likely on his way to the treasure right now. That's what he really wanted. Reese would have to check into the hotel later. Now he had to race back to the beach and keep the German from retrieving what had been bought at such a great price.

As he pulled himself up from his chair, the cantina's door opened and Klein reappeared. "Henry, what's keeping you so long? I saved your life, and you just sit around here waiting for someone to investigate. I think it's time we find your friends and get to that hotel. You look like you need to rest up a bit."

"You *are* on my side," a shocked Reese announced.

"I figured that was pretty obvious by now."

THE 13TH FLOOR

CHAPTER 9

Friday, July 24, 1942
8:11 p.m.
The Grant Hotel, Washington, DC

Melon set Helen Meeker's appearance before the Congressional Intelligence Committee for 9:00 a.m. on Monday morning, and everyone in Washington was talking about it. Even more troubling than testifying before the intelligence committee, she was completely in the dark on the mission to Mexico. She wondered if Gail Worel had finally met up with the love of her life, and if Clay Barnes was now piloting them back to the United States. A part of her was happy for the British woman, but perhaps an even larger part was jealous. Gail was reclaiming love while Meeker would never see Henry Reese again. And what had he been lost for? Nothing! With her cover blown, her future was more than likely being a thorn in the President's side rather than a woman defined by her war service. She pushed her mind away from what had been lost just long enough to once more consider what she was soon facing.

What did Melon really know about Helen? Had he managed to meet with Grace Lupino before she died? And if that were the case, did this mean the senator also knew about Becca and Clay?

After finishing the last of her roast beef, Meeker pushed away from the table and headed to the room that had been booked for her at the hotel. Strolling through the Grant's large lobby, she stopped at the elevators and punched the up button. A few moments later, a door opened, and a uniformed young woman asked, "Going up?"

"Yes, 14th floor," Meeker announced as she stepped into the empty lift. A second later, just before the door closed, another person joined them. In a soft voice, he echoed her choice of floors.

As the elevator slowly rose, Meeker watched its lights tick off the floors. It was then, for the first time in her life, she noted there was no 13th floor. As the woman brought the car to a stop on fourteen, Meeker popped the question that likely everyone asked.

"What happened to the 13th floor?"

"There isn't one," the attendant explained. "None of the Grant Hotels have one. In fact, most skyscrapers don't. Most people won't rent out rooms on that floor because they consider it unlucky. Same is true for office space. So they just pretend they aren't there, even though I guess you are actually staying on the 13th because your room is on the 14th. If that makes any sense."

"People are that superstitious?" Meeker inquired.

"You wouldn't believe it if I told you," the woman replied.

As the doors opened, Meeker stepped out into the hall and headed to Room 1437. The man who had joined them on the car followed a few steps behind. As she stopped and fished the key from her purse, he strolled on by and around a corner. Once again alone, she turned the lock, opened the door and stepped in. An instant later, she felt cold steel against her back.

"Just keep going," a voice suggested. "I'll close the door."

She walked into the dark room and waited. Only when she heard the door close, and her uninvited guest flipped on the overhead light, did she turn around. She shrugged as she noted the man's unshaven face and hollow eyes.

"The whole world's looking for you," Meeker cracked. "Considering the newshounds and most of the nation knows you're after me makes your choice of rooms stupid. Besides, according to hotel rules, this a single."

"You always did have a sharp wit," he snapped, "even when we first met in the British Embassy."

"We guessed right, didn't we?" she noted. "You are Alistar."

"Everything you released to the press was spot on," he admitted.

"With a million sets of eyes knowing your face and lusting for that huge reward, you don't have a chance. Your life is likely numbered in hours ... days at the most."

"Well, your life is now numbered in minutes. So, I will have one bit of satisfaction before they catch me."

"Can I sit down?" she asked. "Your threats are putting me to sleep."

"Yeah," he agreed, "but leave your purse on the table. I don't want you anywhere close to that Colt."

Meeker dropped her bag on the entry table and walked to the suite's couch. After sitting, she crossed her legs and waited for Fister to make the next move. As she dangled the heel of her pump from her right foot, he made his pitch.

"I should have killed you a hundred times. If I had, I would be walking free right now."

"Well," she pointed out, "you'd stand a lot better chance at living longer if you hadn't come to Washington. That was pretty dumb, Alistar, even by your standards. Have you been hitting that crazy water again?"

"I was already here when the news broke," Fister explained. "I was keeping an eye on someone else. If she strayed, I was supposed to knock her off."

"Grace Lupino?" Meeker asked. "I'm guessing she strayed a bit beyond your control."

He walked over to a wooden desk chair, turned it around and sat with his arms draped over the back. Still, the forty-five loosely held in his right hand remained pointed in her direction.

"I wasn't here for Grace. I didn't know where she was. When she saw me, she thought I was Reggie. I kind of played along. Then she explained what she had done. How she'd sold you out for thirty thousand. At first, I thought it was funny, but then as she went on, I realized she had sold me out too."

"There was no mention of you in the *Washington Sun*."

"You don't get it," Fister barked, "she didn't get the money from the newspaper. She got it from some congressman. She went to him with the goods, and he bought her off. He was the one who fed the *Sun* the story. That was to bring you out of hiding."

Meeker shook her head; the mystery had been solved. Melon might not know about all their cases, but he surely had enough ammunition to reframe the President as a man who had no respect for the rules of a democracy. Her testifying on the Hill would be the final nail in that coffin. After Monday's hearing, the OSS, Secret Service, FBI, and pretty much everyone in both houses would be demanding FDR relinquish some of his power. He would likely survive, but his presidency would be deeply weakened.

"Did you kill Grace?" Meeker asked.

"No," Fister quickly replied. "When she figured out I wasn't Reggie, she told me she was going to make everything all right and took off. I lost her in the mass of people at Grand Central Station."

"So," the woman mused, "who killed her?"

"I don't know, but I am going to take credit for killing you. They can even put that on my tombstone."

She smiled. In truth, death might be a better option than having to be grilled by Melon. Without Helen on the stand and with his source dead, his case might just fall apart.

"How do I look?" she asked.

"What do you mean?"

"Just answer the question. How do you think I look?"

"In truth, you're look as beautiful as you did the first night we met. The blue dress you're wearing perfectly matches your eyes. I like that you've let your hair grow out. But why is this important now?"

"Someone is going to find my body," Meeker explained, "and I'd like to think I looked my best in the minutes before I died. I'm not trying to be vain, I just don't want to look tired and used up. And in truth, that's the way I feel."

"You don't," he assured her, "you're still a knockout!"

"I see you have a silencer on that gun," Meeker noted.

"This is not a suicide mission," he explained. "I'm still going to do my best to get away. But if I'm going to die, I want to make sure that you go first. By the way, I still don't understand how that gator didn't get you."

She laughed. New Orleans seemed liked a million years ago. In some ways, it was. A lot had changed since then.

"Alistar, do you ever regret what you've done?"

"No," he almost proudly admitted, "I was a superman for a while. I lived like a king. My life might be short, but I didn't die in a foxhole." He pushed out of the chair and stood. "Now, Helen, if you know any prayers, you might want to say them. I'm going to turn the radio on, and as soon as it warms up, I'll do what I came here to do."

CHAPTER 10

Friday, July 24, 1942
8:42 p.m.
The Grant Hotel, Washington, DC

Someone should write a song called "It's Now or Never." The lyrics could have been the theme for Helen Meeker's life since she joined the President's service. Yet, as the radio warmed up, it was Woody Herman's, "Blues In The Night" that filled the room. That wasn't a bad song to die to.

Meeker almost gleefully noted, "Senator Melon is going to be *so* disappointed that I won't be honoring his party invitation." She then looked into Fister's brooding eyes and smiled. "Do you want me standing or sitting?'

"You're not posing for a portrait," he cracked.

"Well," she shot back, "this is my final sitting."

"Just stay there," he suggested.

There were twelve feet between Meeker and Fister. It would likely take her a second or two to push off the divan and then another four steps to launch her body into his. He was a pro, so during that time, he could likely squeeze off, at least, five rounds. She figured the odds of all those shots hitting her were about fifty-fifty. Still, if she managed to make it halfway to the shooter before she died, it would be a miracle. Yet, it was better to go out fighting than just waiting around like a sitting duck.

She eyed Fister as he raised the gun and set the sights. His hand was trembling slightly. As he tried to steady himself, she dug her heels into the wood floor and sprang forward. Keeping her head down, she'd made two long steps when she heard a click and a muffled explosion. A split second later, she realized he had missed. Two more steps found her shoulder pushing into his gut. Wrapping her arms around him, she drove Fister into the wall. When he hit, she saw the gun slip from his hand and fall to the floor. Dropping to her knees, she grabbed the revolver, rolled over and sprang to her feet. After getting her bearings, she turned to face him. Fister was lying in a fetal position on the floor; his eyes open but not seeing. There was also a bullet hole in his forehead.

Her nemesis was dead. How?

Whirling, the gun poised for action, she glanced toward the suite's bedroom. Standing there, a revolver in her gloved hand, was Teresa Bryant.

"What are you doing here?" Meeker demanded.

"Before I answer that," Bryant suggested, "I think you need to thank me."

"Yeah, I guess I do. Thanks. Now back to my question of what you're doing in my room dressed like the Queen of Sheba?"

"Oh, this old thing," Bryant said with a smile, "my normal stuff was at the cleaners. More about why I'm dressed like a hopeful débutante in a few minutes, I'm here to give you a file that'll likely solve a few of your problems. I'd been waiting in your room for about ten minutes when you and our friend arrived."

"How did you get in?" Meeker asked.

"You think Becca Bobbs is the only one who can pick locks? Now, I'd rather not look at our guest, so why don't we move back into the bedroom."

Bryant led the way and took a seat in the room's lone chair. Meeker followed, and after setting Fister's gun on the end table took a place on the bed.

"See that large file you set the gun on?" the visitor asked.

Meeker glanced over, slipped the folder from under the revolver and opened it. On the first page was written ... Andrew Melon."

"Helen, you now have all the dirt J. Edgar Hoover has on the senator. Study that file and then set an appointment to go see him one-on-one. You won't have to use a third of the material you possess to convince him to drop the hearings."

"But ..."

"How? Well, I obviously lifted it from Hoover's private files. He's out of town and so it won't be missed for a few days. But I will need it back by Monday night."

Meeker shook her head. "Why are you doing this?"

"That's the best question you asked," Bryant answered. "For the moment, let's just say I didn't want to see you pay for doing the right thing. And, I want you to hear this very closely, you owe me, and I will cash in at some point. Now do you have any other questions?"

"Yeah."

"What?"

"How do you keep from catching cold in something that low cut?"

Bryant grinned, "I was one of the decorations at one of Gertrude Root's parties. It seems Root wanted me there to charm congressmen into supporting certain programs her husband is championing and my boss, Hoover, wants me there to try to pry information out of those same people. The irony being that one of the men who followed me everywhere was none other than Andrew Melon."

"I'll bet you are good at that," Meeker suggested.

"Let's just say the dress worked. Now we have one more problem to deal with."

"Fister."

"Yeah," Bryant agreed. "Well, you set him up at the press conference. Thus, it makes sense he would want to go after you. As he was wanted dead or alive, the fact his heart is no longer beating won't matter to anyone. And if you donate the reward to charity, you could elevate yourself from national hero to saint."

"Ah," Meeker pointed out, "we have a problem. I didn't kill him, you did."

"That's no problem at all," Bryant noted. "I'll leave my gun. Just tell the police it was his and you wrestled it from him. I'll take Fister's, so there are no other questions. Give me about five minutes before you call the cops. Oh, and make sure no one sees that file."

"One lie after another," Meeker mumbled.

"Sometimes we have to lie for the right reasons."

"Miss Bryant."

"Call me Teresa."

"Teresa, do you have any idea who killed Grace Lupino?"

"It's the last entry in the files," came the quick reply.

"Why would he kill her?"

"She knew too much about him. Lupino would have drained him for the rest of his life. You see, Melon uses people and disposes of them. Ironically, he tried to frame Dick Diamond while the senator is actually the Judas in this story. Now give me five minutes and call in a homicide captain named Green. He will buy everything you tell him. Oh, there is one more thing."

"What?"

Bryant walked up to Meeker, grabbed the shoulder of her dress and ripped it down to the waist. She then pulled back and landed a blow to Meeker's chin knocking her back onto the bed.

"Now, they'll believe you were in a fight for your life," Bryant announced.

Picking up Fister's gun from the table, the visitor dropped the weapon into her purse, swept out of the room by the dead man's body and through the door. Meeker followed her, locked the door and turned back to the man who had wanted to kill her. As she rubbed her chin, she couldn't help but feel a little sorry for him.

THE 13TH FLOOR

CHAPTER II

Friday, July 24, 1942
9:42 p.m.
The Casa Grande, Progreso, Mexico

Whoever named the Casa Grande Hotel had painted a verbal picture that didn't hold up to the facts. The place was a dump. It would have taken at least three maids working for four weeks to remove the top layer of dust. After that, an archaeological team might be needed to identify what the maids uncovered.

Becca Bobbs approached the main desk. As she waited for the manager to finish a phone call, Worel, Barnes, and Vance joined her.

"Can I help you?" the manager asked in English.

"We're here to meet with a Mr. Carl Jenkins."

"You are?" the manager answered. "I'm not sure we have someone by that name here."

Clay Barnes yanked out his old Secret Service badge. "Let me explain something to you. We're here in an officially capacity with the United States War Department. It is vital we take Mr. Jenkins back to our country as soon as possible."

"That may be," the manager replied, "but I do not just give out room numbers to just anybody. Mr. Jenkins told me he was not to be disturb no matter who was calling."

Bobbs frowned, "Who is on first base." A confused look greeted her response so she tried another tact. Pulling out a picture she showed it to the manager. He shrugged. She then laid a twenty-dollar bill on the counter.

"I think I might be remembering the room number, at least, the first part of it."

Another twenty was dropped over the first one.

"It was one something ..."

Bobbs looked from the manager to Vance. The portly private eye reached into his pocket and yanked out a thirty-eight. As the suddenly nervous hotel manager looked from the gun to the money, Vance quietly demanded, "What's the room number?"

"One-seven," came the quick response.

"You keep an eye on him," Bobbs suggested, "Gail, Clay, and I will go up and retrieve our guests."

With Bobbs leading the way, the trio walked down a long hall and made a right. Four doors later they reached their destination. As the others fingered their guns, the blonde knocked on the door and announced, "It's your ride."

"Becca?"

"And friends."

The door swung open, and a smiling Henry Reese stepped out. He reached for Bobbs but stopped when he saw the woman standing just to her right.

"Gail!"

Pushing the American woman to the side, Reese and Worel's arms found each other and then a second later, their lips their lips met. As their kiss lingered, a suddenly uncomfortable Bobbs looked away. That was when she noted the other man now standing in the door.

"You must be Miss Bobbs," the stranger announced with a thick German accent. "And this has to be Clay Barnes. I've heard a great deal about you in the past day. I'm Fitz Klein, formally of the German Navy."

Bobbs looked to Barnes and back to Klein before awkwardly announcing, "I guess it's nice to meet you."

"Don't worry," the German assured them, "he has my gun, and I really am on your side. By the way, I understand you, Mr. Barnes, Miss Worel, and I have something in common. We are now all considered to be dead."

Bobbs glanced back to the still lip-locked Worel and shrugged, "Actually, she and the man in the lobby are still technically alive. But if she doesn't come up for air soon, she might suffocate before we can get you and Henry back to the States."

Reese finally released his grip on Worel, and as their lips parted, he looked back toward the German. "Didn't I tell you she was beautiful?"

"Actually, your words didn't fully do her justice."

"Well," Worel chimed, "I like that!"

"We need to get moving," Bobbs suggested. "The plane is fueled up and ready to go. Do you have the goodies?"

"We dug them up this morning. Everything is in that chest over there. I'm guessing Churchill and the King will be very happy. And Fritz has a story that's a horrifying reminder of why we need to get this war over with as quickly as possible."

"Let's grab the stuff and get moving," Barnes suggested. "We've got a car out front."

Barnes took the trunk while Bobbs retrieved a Nazi-issued backpack and led the way to the lobby. When the group moved past the desk, Vance slipped his gun back into his pocket and joined them. Once outside, they piled into a fifteen-year-old Buick and, with Barnes driving, did a U-turn and headed south.

"The plane is on a private strip about five miles away," Bobbs explained. "We borrowed the car, and we really need to get it back before the owner figures a way out of the handcuffs we allowed him to borrow."

"I tried to tell them it wasn't cricket," Worel added.

"Things just got a bit complicated," Barnes announced. "We appear to have company."

Bobbs, who was sitting in the back seat with Vance and Klein, looked over her shoulder. There were two cars closing fast.

"Local police?" Reese asked.

"No," Vance explained, "We've already bribed them. This is likely someone who saw us carry that chest from the hotel."

"Banditos," Bobbs whispered. "This area is thick with them."

"I'm sorry to say this old car is not going to outrun them," Barnes noted. "So how do you want to play it?"

"I'm not real big on having a shoot-out in a foreign country," Bobbs announced.

"Well, they're about to pull up beside us," Barnes explained, "so you don't have much time to come up with another plan."

"They won't use guns unless they have to," Vance cut in. "What they'll do is pull in front of us and force us to the side of the road."

"And you know this how?" Worel asked.

"It's standard operating procedure for Mexican bandits," the detective casually replied. "Just take my word for it. They have no interested in using their weapons."

The words had no sooner escaped his lips than a string of bullets raked the old Buick's hood.

"Where did you get that information, Dizzy?" Barnes yelled as he fought to keep the car heading straight down the deeply rutted road.

"Gangbusters."

"Another example of the power of radio," Bobbs noted.

"How many do you see in the two cars?" an agitated Reese barked.

"Eight," Bobbs called out.

"Okay," Reese suggested, "they have the advantage. Clay, slow up and pull over. Keep your guns ready but hidden. Maybe we can do a little negotiating."

As the team found their guns and stuffed them into their pockets, Barnes slowed the car and eased to a stop along the road. The banditos pulled one car in front of the ancient Buick and the other beside it. A voice from the front car called out in Spanish for the passengers to get out with their hands up.

"Follow my lead," Reese suggested as he pushed the door open and stepped out into the darkness. As he shot his hands skyward, he asked, "Do you speak English?"

"Of course," came the reply from a short man with a dark, shabby beard. "I speak many languages. It helps in my business."

"And that business is?" Bobbs asked.

"The business of taking your money and reinvesting it in my country."

"We are a little light on cash," Reese suggested, "but we will give you what we have if you'll let us go."

"My letting you go depends upon how much a little is. If a little is a lot, then your chances of walking away from this are much greater."

The leader was joined by the other seven members of the band, each dressed in light colored slacks and shirts. They also wore sandals and carried weapons ranging from a couple of rifles to a shotgun, two fairly modern revolvers, and a pair of six-shooters that were likely sixty years old.

"Pedro," the leader ordered, "Check their pockets. Jose, you search the car."

As the two men stepped forward, Reese barked, "We will be happy to empty our pockets for you, but I really don't want your men searching our women."

"We are the ones with the guns," the leader explained, "so we make the rules."

"But," Reese cut in as he dropped his arms and nonchalantly reached into his pocket, "I am the one with the hand grenade, and that trumps your guns." The American casually pulled the pin while holding the trigger closed. "Now, here is the way we are going to play this. Your boys lay down their guns, or I'll toss this little potato to you. If you're really quick, you might be able to get about five feet away before he blows up. But sadly that won't be far enough."

"You are playing a dangerous game," the leader coldly stated. "If I shoot you, your friends will blow up. In that case, I think we could run fast enough to escape."

"There is one flaw in that plan," Bobbs announced.

"And what is that, señorita?"

"The chest," she smugly explained. "I'm sure you saw us take it out of the hotel and bring it to our car. I'm also pretty sure that's why you followed us. That trunk contains enough dynamite to blow this section of Mexico to Cuba. If that grenade goes off, so do the explosives. Then all of us will then die."

"You're bluffing," the bandit announced.

"Try us," Bobbs dared.

No one spoke for a full minute. Finally, the gang's leader lowered his gun, and his men followed his lead.

"What's your name?" Reese demanded.

"Hector."

"Hector," the American suggested, "why don't you get into the Buick with us. Then have your men move both of your cars off to the side of the road."

"Where do I sit?" Hector asked. "The car is pretty full."

"On the dynamite chest on the back floorboard," Bobbs barked. "If they start shooting, I want you to be first one to feel the impact."

Reese stood in the open with the grenade until his team and Hector were back in the Buick, and the other two cars had moved. As Barnes fired up the old Buick, Reese jumped in and then slid the pin back into place. A few moments later, they were bumping back down the road. They'd had only traveled about a quarter mile when the banditos began to follow them.

When they arrived at the small dirt strip airfield, Barnes pulled the Buick beside the DC-2. Within seconds, the visitors to Mexico poured out of the vehicle and dashed to the plane. This time, it was Vance who carried the trunk.

Holding Hector by the shirt collar, Bobbs pushed the bandit through the plane's door and into the cabin. Reese, the last one in, yanked the door shut at the same moment Barnes started the left motor. Within thirty seconds, the right one caught and the aircraft began to rumble down the strip.

Without their leader, the banditos initially looked lost, but as they watched the DC-2 come to life, they woke up. Guns blazing, they followed behind the big black bird in their cars. At least three rounds tore through the cabin just above Hector's head, causing him to curse in Spanish and fall to the floor. Except for the pilot, everyone else quickly joined him.

As the sound of the gunfire grew distant, and the plane's wheels left the ground, the party relaxed and found their seats. The only exception was Hector; he remained on the floor and, based on his whispers, he might have been praying.

"What do we do about him?" Vance asked.

"I doubt if he has a passport," Bobbs noted, "so we can't take him back to the States." She paused and smiled. "Ask Clay to keep this crate over land for a while."

Moving to the plane's tail, she grabbed a bag and returned to the cabin. Yanking Hector off the floor, she pulled his arms out to his side and slipped two straps over the man's shoulders. She then fastened a buckle in the front.

"What is this?" Hector demanded.

Bobbs didn't bother to reply. Instead, she marched the bandit back to the door and signal for Reese to open it. After it was pulled open, the woman looked down into the Mexican night.

"You're going to throw me out?" a trembling Hector asked.

"You were going to kill us," Bobbs noted.

"Actually," he explained, "I don't really like to kill. I avoid it whenever possible. I'm just an honest bandit, that's all. And I think I could be persuaded to give that up very soon. My grandfather has a goat farm, and he has asked me to run it for him. If I promised to do that would you let me go?"

"Sounds like a great idea," Bobbs noted. "Who's got twenty bucks?"

Vance reached into his pocket and retrieved two tens. The woman took the money, stuffed it into Hector's pocket and then pushed him to where he was standing with his back to the open door. Shouting so she could be heard, Bobbs announced, "Hector, count to three and pull this cord. Say Maria before each number so you don't count too fast."

"And what happens then?" the frightened man asked.

"A chute will open, and you will float down to the ground. If the first chute doesn't open, then pull this second cord. Do you understand?"

"Couldn't I just go with you? I have a cousin in America. He lives in Arizona."

"No," Bobbs yelled over the rush of air, "your country needs you."

She smiled, nodded and moved the man's trembling hand to the cord. Then, with no warning, Bobbs pushed Hector out the door. For a few seconds, she heard his screams, but when the chute opened there were cries of thankfulness.

"That was not nice," Worel pointed out after the door was once again secure.

"It was a lot better than he deserved," Bobbs rationalized. "Now let's get back to our base and sort things out. Helen's likely in a bunch of trouble, and we might just have to help her."

CHAPTER 12

Friday, July 24, 1942
11:58 p.m.
Over the Gulf of Mexico

Still dressed in the black slacks and shirt she had worn on the mission, Becca Bobbs pulled her blonde hair into a ponytail and, from her seat at the rear of the DC-2, studied Henry Reese and Gail Worel. The pair seemingly couldn't take their eyes off each other. They acted more like two high school kids on their first date than two veterans of armed conflict. Just watching their obvious attraction left Bobbs feeling very uneasy.

"I have heard a great deal about her," Fritz Klein leaned closer and softly announced.

Bobbs looked to her left and admitted, "She's talked a lot about him too."

"Does it bother you?" the German asked.

She shrugged, "I'm not sure it bothers me as much as it leaves me numb. It just doesn't make sense. He was so hung up on another woman before he ..." She paused.

Reese died. She saw him die. The Nazis had gunned him down. So how was he four rows ahead of her in the plane?

"I think you were about to say," Klein chimed in, "before he died. While we were waiting for you, he told me about that. It was faked. The men who supposedly killed him were shooting over his head. They worked for the underground. It was all elaborate stunt that was played out just so you and everyone else would believe he was dead."

"It was all a lie," she groaned.

"No," Klein argued, "The mission wasn't a lie. It was real, but he was sent to stay behind. The best way for you to accept that essential part of the plan was for you to see him die."

"It was cruel," she suggested.

"War is cruel," he added. "Let me tell you how cruel it really is. Sometime in the next week or two, my wife and children will be told that I am dead. They will need to believe it in order for them to be safe."

"That's not fair to them."

The German nodded. "Would it be better for them to know that I'm a traitor? Can you imagine what the SS would do to them if they realized I had come over to your side? The great German U-boat commander, the man Hitler himself decorated, and the pride of the Nazi Navy meeting with your side and giving them information that is so secret only a handful of people in Germany know about it. Once more I ask you, what would the SS do with my family if they knew that?"

Bobbs had an idea of what would happen, but it wasn't something she wanted to consider. Instead, she turned her eyes back to the front of the plane to once more observe the reunited lovers. As she continued to study Henry and Gail, she posed a question that perhaps even Klein couldn't answer.

"Why did you turn?"

"I can tell you don't approve," the German noted. "It's written all over your face, and I can hear it your tone."

She turned to look him in the eye. "I'm sure it is. And I don't like what Henry did either. If he had stayed where he'd belonged, then he and Helen would be together."

"You don't know that," Klein argued.

"At least," she offered, "he wouldn't be with her."

"So the fact that he is happy," the German noted, "bothers you. You don't want him to be in love."

"It's not that," she argued, "it's just I don't want my friend to be hurt. She's been hurt enough."

"You have to understand," Klein suggested, "Henry was dead to your friend and that made her dead to him. On top of that, he was constantly living on the edge between life and death. He was always one bullet away from the end. So unless you're married and are just trying to survive until you can get home, you live in the moment. And that's what he was doing. And in one of those moments, he fell in love with a woman, who, like him, was living in the moment. That's war."

Bobbs turned her eyes back to Klein, "But do you know what losing him twice will mean to my friend? Do you understand what it will be like for her to have her heart broken again? I mean her entire world has fallen apart. Everything she lived for is gone. And now, the love of her life comes back, and she has lost him to another woman … a woman she knows."

"No one ever said life was fair," he suggested, "and there are far worse things than losing a man to another woman."

The blonde raised her eyebrows. "Such as?"

Klein turned his face to look out the plane's small window and sadly shook his head. Bobbs let him stare into the darkness for several moments, but her eyes never left him.

"You'll likely see your family when this mess is over," the woman suggested when she grew tired of the silence.

He continued to study the blackness of the Gulf and shrugged. "Maybe I will. But that won't fix what's eating at my gut. A lifetime of living won't do that."

"Then I guess I need to ask again, why did you turn on your country?"

He shifted to face her. "I didn't. My country turned on me. And living wasn't in my plans. I would rather have gone down with my ship. Your friend could have delivered my information to your intelligence department as well I could have. He just made a mistake and saved my life. Time will tell if I owe him for that. After all, dead I was a man with a country, but alive I don't have one. Which is worse?"

Bobbs shook her head. "I never met a man who regretted having his life saved."

"You have now. Maybe in time, I'll change my mind."

"So," the woman asked, "what's your plan?"

"If your government allows it, Henry will take me back with him. I'll fight for the underground. In the process, he thinks we can get my family out of Germany. If we can do that, then I'll be thankful for him saving my life."

She nodded and looked back to Reese and Worel, whose head was now on his shoulder. If he were going back overseas, maybe Helen wouldn't find out Henry was alive. At the very least, she wasn't going to tell him.

Bobbs laid her head back on the seat. She was exhaust-ed. Perhaps a bit of sleep would put this whole mess into perspective.

THE 13TH FLOOR

CHAPTER 13

Saturday, July 25, 1942
4:15 p.m.
Washington home of Senator Andrew Melon

Andrew Melon's house was a colonial style, white brick monster setting in the middle of grounds that could have doubled for a golf course. Armed with only her purse and guile, Helen Meeker drove her 1936 yellow Packard through the front gate and up to the home's massive front double doors. Stepping from the car, she smoothed her jade green suit, adjusted her hat and marched forward. After she rang the bell, only a few seconds elapsed before the senator himself pulled the huge, mahogany entry open.

"Why, Miss Meeker," he quipped, "I really don't think our visiting before we meet on Monday is appropriate. So tell me, why did you call and set up this little date?"

Melon was smug, confident, and arrogant, a combination that for some reason made him a favorite in the southern state he called home, but it turned Meeker's stomach. Yet, as the visitor studied the man's beady eyes, plump cheeks, and thick lips, she smiled. At more than three hundred pounds, he was a big man, and she'd always found it pleasant to bring someone like that down.

"I'm not here to make a deal," she calmly replied, "and I'm not here to talk about our case. This visit is on another matter altogether, and it does involve national security."

He stepped to one side and grinned. "You likely do know a few things I need to know. I'm glad you're ready to share them. Perhaps I can return the favor by taking it easy on you this Monday."

"Maybe you can," she announced as she strolled past the senator and for the second time in just a few hours walked into the home's two-story foyer. After Melon closed the door, she asked, "Are we alone?"

"Yes."

"Good," she replied.

"So that's what this is about," he sniped. "Do you think you can use your physical gifts to win me over?"

"Could I?" Meeker cooed.

Melon grinned like a child about to meet Santa. "The master bedroom is down the hall, last door on the right."

After stifling a laugh, Meeker turned to her host and shook her head. "Before we move things that far, why don't we visit in your study?" Her host looked to a door on the near right. She followed his gaze before suggesting, "Senator, why don't you lead the way?"

The study, which likely served as his office, was, at least, twenty by thirty feet. The walls were lined with bookshelves and to the right were a couch, two high-backed leather chairs, and a large table. To the left was a desk the size of a small yacht. Melon opted for one of the chairs and Meeker chose to sit directly across from him. She observed his eyes as she crossed her left leg over her right. This was a man who assumed he had Meeker exactly where he wanted-ed.

"You are a beautiful woman," he gasped.

"Thank you," she announced, momentarily acting as if she appreciated his lustful gaze.

"I must commend you on bringing down Alistar Fister," he said, his eyes still locked on her legs. "That will make it a bit more difficult for me to nail your hide to the wall at the hearings. After all, the country is seeing you as both a victim and hero. Of course, they don't know what I know."

"I really don't care what you know," Meeker explained.

"You mean you're ready to come over to my side?" he asked hopefully.

"No," she assured him. "I'm ready for you to see things my way. Now, listen and take notes. The President was not going behind your back; he just recognized the various intelligence agencies were so jealous of each other, they wouldn't get on the same page. They were all in a race to outdo the other one. Hoover's the worst and, at times, he really can't be trusted."

"Those are dangerous words," Melon noted.

"Maybe," she agreed, "but I have come to understand something. Even in war, this city is all about power—who has it, who controls it and who can best use it. And you know that better than anyone."

"You don't get to my position without understanding that simple fact," he admitted. "But it really doesn't make any difference what Roosevelt's motives were; I can use this to paint him as a megalomaniac who can't be trusted. That's all that matters to me."

"And you will use this lie to pave your run to the White House?" Meeker asked.

"Lie is a strong word."

"You're right," she agreed, "and all we really need to deal with today is the truth."

The senator laughed, "Such as the fact you ran a clandestine operation outside the bounds of US law, thus making your boss into a dictator rather than an elected president."

Meeker grinned, uncrossed her legs, stood and walked over to the window where she spent a few moments in silence pretending to look out at the grounds. As she expected, Melon followed. Standing just behind her, he rested his meaty hands on her shoulders. As he began to squeeze, she whispered, "You seem to have something on your mind."

The senator edged closer, his considerable stomach now pushing into her back. "You must have it on your mind as well."

"Not sure I could follow in the footsteps of Joan Ridell."

Those eleven words caused the man to instantly freeze. While his hands still rested on her shoulders, they no longer moved.

"What?" The word seemed to almost catch in his throat as he spoke.

"Or," Meeker continued, "Carole Light, Mira Close, and Beth Marks."

Melon's hands dropped to his side, and his guest turned and walked back to her chair. As the large man stood mute, she reached for her purse and yanked out a large brown envelope. Holding it in her right hand, she marched to his desk and fanned a series of photographs beside a brass table lamp. She then turned back to her host and grinned. "I think you will want to see these."

Melon, sweat obvious on his brow and suddenly looking a decade older than his fifty years, slowly ambled to the spot and studied the black and white images. As he did, the color drained from his face, and his jaw fell slack. He never looked up as he whispered, "Where did you get these?"

"They're from J. Edgar Hoover's private collection. He has many more, and now, the President has copies as well. I can easily make sure the newspapers and your wife see them too. I really think the photography is quite good. Those pictures show a side of you the voters have never seen."

"How?" His question came out in a barely audible whisper.

"Your lust obviously doesn't begin and end with power," she suggested. "By the way, I also have documentation of all the kickbacks you received from contractors for making sure their companies got first shot at certain programs when your state was in the middle of the Depression. You literally took food off the table of thousands of poor people when you did that. And let's not even go to the place where you sold your soul for cash from defense contractors. I can pretty much tie you to breaking every commandment. That won't fly too well in the Bible Belt during your next election, but it does have the elements of a novel that would be banned in Boston."

"You wouldn't actually use this material?" he asked.

"You seem shocked," she laughed. "I mean it's fine for you to stretch the truth and even employ lies about me to make the President look bad, but you believe I wouldn't use the truth to derail your ambitions. As you and I both know, this is about power."

His shoulders slumping, he moaned, "Everyone here does what I did."

"I don't care to expose them," Meeker replied, "just you. Now go back to that chair and sit down. I'm going to really get to the dirt."

Like a whipped dog, he followed her commands. When he was once more seated, she continued.

"Grace Lupino was your source."

He nodded.

"She knew enough to hatch your plans to start a run to the White House. As I understand it, you paid her thirty thousand to sell me out."

Melon explained, "There is no reason to lie now. You seem to know it all. A nightclub owner, Dick Diamond, told me just a bit of her story over drinks. It seems she had run out of money when her boyfriend disappeared, and Diamond was helping her hide and pay bills. She'd spilled the yarn to him. Lupino didn't realize it, but this wasn't about you, not that I didn't enjoy bringing you down. I just wanted the goods on Roosevelt. I'd been shopping for that angle for years."

"Yeah, that makes sense," Meeker acknowledged. "So what did Diamond get for bringing Grace to you?"

"The same," Melon admitted, "thirty grand."

The woman crossed her arms as she put the information together with what she already had learned from the files. "So you met with Lupino, got the information she had, which was just enough to make things look much worse than they really were. Thanks to the planted newspaper story, you flushed me out into the open where you could put me on trial before the whole country."

"Pretty much," the senator noted. "I have strong connections at the *Sun*, they love gossip and dirt, so it wasn't that hard."

"But," Meeker noted, "then things went south. When she saw what you were doing, Lupino suddenly wanted out of the deal. She gave you the cash back and swore she was lying."

"How could you know that?" he demanded.

"You have a slush fund, and Hoover knows about it. You took out sixty grand and then, a day later, dropped thirty back into it. When you told me about the payment to Diamond, tonight I was able to balance your books."

"But there is no way …"

"No way anyone could know about it?" Meeker asked. "There shouldn't be, but there are times when you drink too much, especially around beautiful women. And one of them worked for Hoover."

"The dark-haired brunette?"

"Her name is Teresa Bryant. You got drunk and bragged about your power and a special fund you have."

"But I didn't tell her …" Melon argued.

Meeker cut him off. "You didn't tell where the money was or who was your banker. Is that what you're saying?"

"Yes. She couldn't have known."

The senator's houseguest smiled. "People say things without speaking all the time."

"Not me."

"Okay," she grinned, "you keep a large amount of cash in the safe in this very room." While Melon shook his head, she studied his eyes. Turning, she walked directly to the far wall, put her hand on a large framed print of Washington crossing the Delaware and pulled it forward. As she expected, it was on a hinge and behind it was a wall safe."

"How?" he demanded.

"Your head said no," she explained as she walked back over to lean on the desk, "but your eyes went right to the photo before returning to me. That night Teresa Bryant asked how you could trust a man to hold that amount of cash for you, your eyes went directly to your banker, who was also at General Root's party."

"My lord," he whispered.

"You might want to start praying," Meeker continued. "When I applied the heat to your money man, he mentioned another ten grand payment. This morning I tracked down the man who got that money. I think you know Mr. Jack Morello."

If it was possible for Melon's face to grow paler, it did. After taking a deep gulp of air, he seemed to melt into the chair.

"Why did …"

"Why did your banker sell you out?" Meeker finished his question for him. "It's easy. When it comes to saving your skin or his, he opted for the logical course." She smiled before suggesting, "Now let me continue to tell the story of how your life unraveled. The key component in this tale is greed. Greed caused you to make more and more deals, and that meant you had to trust more and more people. You should have considered two things. One: J. Edgar has a naughty and nice list much longer than Santa's, and he and his elves are always watching. The second thing is there were simply too many people paying you too much money. Each of those people were buying your services and thus, they also, when presented with a better deal—

such as not serving prison time—would readily sell you out."

Melon's hands were balled up, and the sweat that had begun on his brow was now dripping down onto his shirt. He already resembled a turkey being basted for Thanksgiving, and it was time to turn up the heat even higher.

"You gave Morello instructions to get rid of Lupino. At first, I couldn't figure out why. She didn't know anything about your under-the-board activities, and no one was going to kick you out of office for paying for information. By the time the payment came out in public, you could have reworked your books, and your slush fund would have stayed hidden. So why did you have to silence her? And then it hit me. It was so obvious I'm surprised I spent an hour looking through your file to figure it out. Do you want to tell me why or should I spell it out?"

"You seem to like talking," Melon snapped, "why don't you go ahead."

"She not only gave you information on my work," Meeker explained, "you demanded more for that thirty grand payment. When she gave you the money back, you realized she would share that bit of extra information with the police."

"So we had sex," he grumbled.

"It wasn't sex," Meeker countered, "the medical examiner found that Lupino had been roughed up pretty good. There was a lot of bruising prior to death. It all suggested rape. If she went public with that story, it would likely end your political career."

"She couldn't have proved it," he argued.

"But you couldn't risk that," Meeker noted. "So you set her up by inviting her to your home again. This time, she thought you were going to apologize and agree not to use the remainder of the information you gave her. Dick Diamond also told her she needed to get the money back from you. So she was coming back to grab the cash as well. This time, she saw it as a way of making you pay for forcing yourself on her."

"You're guessing," Melon argued. "No one is going to buy it either."

"Let me finish the story," Meeker suggested. "When Lupino came to your house that day, you were the perfect gentleman. You likely apologized and agreed to her terms. Then you guided her to the small den you have at the back of this home. When you opened the door, and she saw Morello, she tried to run, but you grabbed her by the wrists, pushed her into the room and slammed the door."

"You're still guessing," the senator suggested.

"No," Meeker assured him, "I'm not. There was deep bruising on her left wrist. It was so deep it left an impression of a ring in that bruise. That ring also left a gash on Lupino's left wrist," She watched as Melon glanced down at his right hand. "Once more, Senator, your eyes have given you away."

He quickly looked back to the woman. "You can't prove any of this."

"Look at your ring again," Meeker ordered. "There are about forty tiny diamonds in the setting that form the letter M."

"It was a gift from my wife," he noted.

"And one of those tiny diamonds is missing," she continued. "If you'd like it back, call Captain Tom Green of Homicide. It seems the medical examiner dug it out of Lupino's wrist."

"That still doesn't tie me to her murder," Melon added.

"Yeah," Meeker agreed, "and Morello didn't immediately admit to actually killing her, he only copped to having you pay him for the job. So the matter of linking you to the homicide was a bit harder. Then it hit me. There was no bullet found at the scene. The slug had gone through Lupino's head. I thought it was a long shot, but I decided it was worth taking. You and Morello are men. When you cleaned up the scene in your den where Lupino was executed, I guessed that neither of you thought to search for the bullet. You just cleaned up the blood."

Melon's eyes darted to his left as if trying peer through a wall.

"Yeah, go ahead and look that way, Senator, because you know what I'm about to tell you. Not finding that bullet was a big mistake.

"When I called this morning, I directly asked that we meet alone and at your home. You readily agreed and gave the staff the day off to ensure our privacy. With your wife gone and no one here to cook for you, you went to your club for lunch. While you were wolfing down a steak, I broke in, photographed the wall and then dug the bullet out of the paneling. When ballistics matched it one of Morello's guns, he caved. He's making a deal right now. Your banker will talk as well. He has already told us he supplied the thirty silver dollars you used to plant suspicion on Dick Diamond. In fact, your fingerprints are actually on a couple of them."

Meeker was guessing on the fingerprints, but she was sure of everything else she had shared. By the expression on the man's face, she was likely right on that point as well.

She allowed him to take inventory for a few moments before pushing ahead.

"Your lust for power pulled me from a position where I was able to do a great deal of good for this country's war effort. As a supposedly dead woman, I could save a lot of lives. In the process, I also lost some people I loved. And if you hadn't been so greedy in your grab for more power, your own corrupt world would still be intact. The bottom line was you messed with the wrong woman."

After slowly pushing off the chair, the senator lurched forward, his hands reaching for Meeker's throat. Because of the desk behind her, she couldn't move fast enough to keep his hands from encircling her throat. As he squeezed and lifted her off the ground, she could feel his breath on her face. Although unable to breathe, she grabbed his flabby cheeks in her hands and dug her nails into the flesh. She then launched her right knee at his gut, but, as if possessed, the big man continued to push. After slapping him hard with her hand, she reached behind to the desk and grabbed a heavy paperweight. Using every ounce of strength she had left, she delivered a blow to the side of Melon's forehead. The wallop stunned him just enough to loosen his grip. Using the desk for leverage, Meeker kicked her feet into his gut, and the man staggered backward. By the time he'd regained his balance, there was a Colt pistol pointed at his head.

"What are you going to do?" Melon demanded.

"Sit down and shut up," she barked.

As he moved back to the chair, Meeker rolled her neck a couple of times to get the blood flowing. Once she'd regained her breath, she walked back over to the senator and, using her left hand, slapped him hard across the cheek.

She then backed up, leaned on the desk and laid out what she expected.

"Here's what's going to happen," she announced, her voice echoing off the walls. "Your last act as a senator will be to laud me as a hero and agree the President forced me underground to protect me from Fister. In other words, you will march in step with the White House. Then you will cancel the hearing. A few days later you will announce that due to health issues created by your weight, you will be forced to resign."

"Is that all?" He sounded surprised.

"No," she firmly added. "We will find out how much money you have taken under the table. Next month, the IRS will file charges of income tax fraud against you. The government will then offer you a deal to testify against the companies that used bribes so you would influence contracts and bids. At that point, you will be allowed to serve a few years in prison and then waltz off to obscurity."

"I can't do that," he protested. "It would ruin my legacy."

"Fine," Meeker replied, "then the homicide department will be visiting you later this evening to arrest you for the rape and murder of Grace Lupino. Because that homicide includes issues dealing with the war effort and, as you have no defense, the penalty will be death. You might want to lose some weight before you sit in the electric chair. Right now, it would be a tight squeeze."

Meeker smiled, lowered her gun and slowly walked toward the door. As she reached for the knob, a meek voice called out, "I wasn't always this way. Just one thing seemed to lead to another."

She turned back to the now defeated man. "What you were doesn't matter. This is about what you've become."

"I'll take the deal," Melon whispered.

"Fine, then make your announcement canceling the hearing by tomorrow at five. If you don't the deal is off."

Not waiting for a reply, Meeker marched out of the house and to her car, slid in, hit the starter and motored off up the lane and out the gate. She might have lost a great deal in the last few days, but at least one man had paid the price. She owed Grace Lupino that much and a great deal more.

CHAPTER 14

Monday, July 27, 1942
9:15 a.m.
WOL Radio, Washington, DC

"This is WOL in Washington with a special report. Via our phone line, we are about to take you live to our White House reporter, Milton Simmons."

Station announcer John Hotchins nodded, pulled back from the main studio mic and looked through the glass to engineer Ralph Atkins. Sitting behind the window, the elderly Atkins, who had been working with WOL since it first went on the air in 1928, flipped a switch and placed his hand on one of the large dials of his soundboard. Listening through his headsets, he checked the level and announced, "Simmons, you're on."

A one-time college sprinter, Milton Simmons was tall, lean and in his thirties. On the surface, he appeared to be the picture of perfect health. Yet, when he moved the results of a car accident were readily apparent. Three years before, his right leg was fractured in five places when his

Nash was broadsided by a Pontiac sedan. But the injury did more than make him 4-F, it handicapped his career as well. The fact he couldn't run made him unfit for front line service in the news corps as well as the military. Thus, he was stuck reporting on the White House's response to war rather than seeing it with his own eyes.

"Thank you, John," Simmons announced as he spoke into a phone just off the White House pressroom. "In what will not come as a surprise to anyone who has been following the national news, President Roosevelt announced today that due to the death of Alistar Fister, the man who tried to assassinate both the President and Prime Minister Winston Churchill, there was no longer any reason to protect Helen Meeker. Meeker, the woman many are now calling the real Wonder Woman, foiled that assassination last spring and this weekend gun downed Public Enemy #1 as he attempted to kill her in her hotel room. Before the *Washington Sun* revealed that Meeker was alive, most thought she had been killed in a March plane crash that took the lives of employees of both the Secret Service and the FBI. We now know that ruse was used to throw the bloodthirsty Fister off her trail. Fister, who was once hailed a British war hero, was, in fact, a double agent working for Nazi Germany.

"Today, I was invited into the Oval Office where the President told four other pool reporters and me that Helen Meeker would now work for him as a presidential private investigator. She would use her intelligence and experience to track down individuals involved in criminal efforts to destabilize the war effort. As is to be expected, news of these upcoming investigations will only be released when the individuals responsible are of no further danger to the American people or our allies.

"In other news, Senator Andrew Melon, who had accused the White House of misusing its authority in allowing Miss Meeker to, as Melon said, 'go rogue,' has completely reversed his position in this matter. While canceling Meeker's appearance before the Senate Intelligence Committee, Melon called Meeker one of finest examples of American womanhood and urged young women everywhere to aspire to follow Meeker's example. Melon then pointed out the news printed in the *Washington Sun* was so erroneously reported, it was an embarrassment to the country's news media. In closing his remarks, Melon hinted at health issues that might not allow him to finish his term. We are currently digging to find out more about that. Now, back to Milton."

From his position in the studio, Simmons looked to Hotchins as he pushed a switch. A second later, the announcer, this time reading from a script, continued his report.

"In other breaking news, the Washington Police announced this morning that the body of a woman found over the weekend in an alley was, in fact, former nightclub singer, Grace Lupino. Homicide Captain Tom Green told this station that a suspect in the woman's murder had been apprehended, and his name would be released within twenty-four hours."

After taking a quick breath, Hotchins continued, "Now it's time to put a platter on the turntable and let WOL spin today's greatest tunes for your listening pleasure. Here is that hot new release from Glenn Miller—'I've Got a Gal in Kalamazoo'."

As Simmons keyed up the sound on the big band hit, Hotchins walked into the control room, lit a cigarette and took a seat beside the engineer. After smoothing his thick, dark hair, he dropped into a chair, propped his feet on a desk and observed, "Right now the battle of New Britain is raging, fighting is heavy in North Africa and German subs are continuing to take a toll on American shipping in the Atlantic. And I'm stuck reporting the news of the death of a nightclub singer who likely was killed by a jilted lover. How fair is that?"

CHAPTER 15

Monday, July 26, 1942
10:15 a.m.
A Farm Outside of Springfield, Illinois

As weekends go, this one had been a nightmare. So, it was an agitated Fredrick Bauer who sipped on lukewarm coffee as he reread the story in the *Springfield Record*. That second reading was even worse than the first. The bad news hadn't changed. Alistar Fister was still dead. Thus, Bauer's prize lab rat would not be coming back to him again. Worse yet, Helen Meeker was alive and being honored as a hero. Then there was Teresa Bryant. He couldn't decide if she was playing on his team or just freelancing.

Bauer was all about control. He always had been. But at this moment, he felt as if he had little control over any facet of his life. Worse yet, a future that had once seemed so assured was now lost in fog as thick as pea soup.

As he drummed his fingers on his office desk, the phone rang. Because of recent events, the normally confident man picked up his private line with more than a bit of apprehension.

"Yes."

"Most people answer with hello."

"Gertrude. Why are you bothering me?"

"Fred, if you've been listening to the radio, you pretty much know your choices of callers has recently diminished by one."

"Yeah, Fister's dead. So what do you need?"

"I don't need anything," the woman assured, "I just wanted you to know that Bryant bit at my offer and is one of my party hostesses. She's playing her role just the way I asked her to. She wore the dress I picked out and got close to the men I told her to charm."

"The men on my list?" Bauer asked.

"Yes, my dear brother." Her reply smacked of sarcasm.

"What about your husband, have you heard any news out of him?"

"If you mean is he talking?" Root exclaimed, "The answer is no! But I did find plans for a troop placement in Africa in our safe and have obtained a list of two secret projects involving aircraft. Those were dropped in the mail today. You know where to look for the microfilm."

"General Delivery and hidden under stamps?"

"At least, your mind is still sharp," she chirped.

"How do you read Bryant?" he asked, shifting the conversation back to his most pressing concern.

"She's just like you described," Root replied, "bright, beautiful, and seemingly with no loyalty to anyone but herself. I've done enough digging to know that J. Edgar hates her but fully understands her usefulness. He will keep her around as long as she does his bidding and her attitude doesn't get in the way of the Bureau's day-to-day business. But if she tries to grab too much power or demand public credit for her work, she will be gone."

"You know that Hoover doesn't respect any woman but his mother," Bauer pointed out.

"Everyone knows that," the woman replied, "but J. Edgar uses women as pawns and tools just like everyone else in Washington."

"I've got news for you," Bauer noted, "They use women that way in Berlin too."

"Well, nevertheless," Root noted, "judging by the way she worked my party, he should keep her around just to use as bait. From what I hear, his secret files can pretty much sink about fifty percent of those in Congress. I'll bet she helps him put more material in those files too. She has that kind of charm."

"What about Meeker?" he asked. "I know what the press is saying, but what's the tone with those in power? Do they respect her?"

"Helen Meeker is nothing more than a distraction," Root suggested. "I've met her, watched her work, and I just don't see her as being much more than FDR's poster girl. Yes, she derailed a few of your operations, but she had help. When she is on her own, she will be nothing more than a woman in over her head trying to survive in a man's world."

"I don't know," he argued, "there's something about her."

"Yeah, she looks like someone you loved a long time again. Between that and your telling me you saw pictures of Bryant from eighty years ago, I'm beginning to wonder if you aren't losing your mind. You need to get a grip. Fred, Hitler doesn't faze you …"

"He's crazy."

"And if you believe the garbage about Bryant, and fall for the allure of Meeker, then you and he are in the same boat. Now stop worrying. Hoover and I will keep Bryant busy. And from here on out Meeker will be followed around by the press. She won't have a moment's peace. In the last few days, her face has become as well-known as Betty Grable's, so there's no place to hide."

"I should have killed them both when I had the chance."

"Of course," Root agreed, "but that's water under the bridge."

"Yes, but remember, Bryant knows where my operation is. She has been here, and she can find her way back."

"If she leaves town," Root replied, "I'll let you know. Now check your mail. Your friends in Germany will pay us dearly for that information. I would like a Monet if you can arrange it. If not that, I guess we can settle for a few more large diamonds."

"Goodbye, Gertrude."

As Bauer dropped the phone back into the receiver, he frowned. Without Fister around to watch Bryant, she was far too dangerous. He couldn't wait any longer, he had to know what she was thinking. Picking up the receiver he contacted the long distance operator.

"Number please."

"I need the FBI. headquarters in Washington, DC."

"To whom do you want to speak?"

"Teresa Bryant."

"And how is this to be billed?"

"To this number."

"Just a minute please."

It was actually more like three minutes when he was finally connected to the woman he both needed and feared.

"Hello."

"It's Bauer."

"Why are you calling me here?"

"Because you don't answer your home phone."

"I'm pretty busy. I actually have a new way to get close to those you want to influence. I'm playing hostess for General Root."

"Fine, but you likely need another injection. So we should meet."

"If you remember, I have access to the FBI lab and can whip up my own drug whenever I want. So, we don't need to meet."

Something had to be done! She couldn't treat him this way!

"Whose side are you on?" Bauer demanded. "I need to know that."

"I'm on my side," came Bryant's ready response. "And with your gunner dead, maybe you need to come to grips that we either work together and share, or we don't work at all. I'm not looking for a boss; I'm looking for a partner. Think about that."

The woman didn't wait for a response.

As the line went dead, Bauer put the phone down and considered what he had been told. That exchange proved Bryant had to be stopped. Thus, it was time to call in a favor. Big Jim O'Toole had the connections and resources to silence the woman forever.

THE 13TH FLOOR

CHAPTER 16

Monday, July 26, 1942
3:30 p.m.
The Oval Office, Washington, DC

It had been a while since Helen Meeker could enter the White House in the middle of the day. As she walked through the historic residence, a host of people rushed up to greet her. They had been her friends, and it was wonderful to have them back. So, in a way, it was good to be home. But what did this new life hold? Would she ever be able to do what she did when everyone thought she was dead, or had her power be severely muted? Thus, she entered the Oval Office looking at a future that was shrouded in impenetrable fog.

The President was behind his desk. Sitting just to his right was her sister. Neither seemed to note Meeker's insecurity. In fact, the President looked like the cat who had just eaten the canary.

"Good to see you," Roosevelt announced. "I'm especially pleased with the information you somehow dug up on a certain senator."

"A soon-to-be-former senator," Meeker noted with a hint of pride.

"Sit down," the President suggested. "I have to go to a briefing in a few minutes, so I need to make this quick."

After Meeker had taken a seat, he continued. "What I'm going to tell you is not something you want to hear. Your team is no longer your team. Bobbs and Barnes will go on doing the work you were assigned without you."

"But …"

"No," the President cut her off with both the word and a wave. "You are alive, and they are considered dead. For a while, the press will be watch your every move. So will the OSS and FBI. So we can't have you being seen with ghosts. For your former team to be effective, you can't associate with them."

"They are my friends," Meeker argued.

"I know," he answered, "but to protect them, the work and even yourself, you need to never go back to the headquarters in Maryland. If on occasion, you and the team are working separately on the same operation, then Alison will serve as the intermediary."

Meeker shook her head. Who would have thought that just being alive would take everything and everyone she cared about away from her?

"The team," the President explained, "will be focused on finding the Declaration of Independence and Magna Charta as well as disposing of all the tainted water that disappeared from New Orleans."

"And what do I do?" Meeker asked.

"I have something in mind for you," he assured her. "Beyond that job, there are some other surprises in store for you as well. So, I order you to relax today. You will soon need your strength and energy on a matter that has Hoover and his boys completely stymied. And I know how you love showing up the FBI. Alison will give you the file on that case. Now, I'm going to roll down the hall and see how the war is going."

After the President pushed his wheelchair out into the hall, Alison got up and closed the door. Her suddenly concerned expression signaled this conversation was going to be anything but light.

"What's troubling you, sis?" Meeker asked. "You look as though you lost your best friend."

"It's about the junket you missed," she began.

"The trip to Mexico to pick up Gail Worel's beau along with a few of the king's trinkets?"

"Ditto."

Suddenly Meeker was deeply concerned. "Did something happen?"

"The show went off script, but the reviews were good."

Meeker shrugged, "I'm guessing that's your way of saying the operation was not without its problems, but the end result was as expected and no lives were lost."

"On target," Alison assured her. "The gig also unwrote an obit."

"What?"

"You aren't the only ghost with substance." She paused, and when Meeker didn't respond, Alison noted, "You aren't digging me, are you?"

"I'm not following the conversation. I wish Becca were here to translate. In fact, if I can't be around Becca, who is going to translate for me when you talk?"

"The man the Brit chick lassoed is the one who stole your heart."

"Alison, you're not making any sense."

"Henry didn't cash it in!" she bluntly announced.

"What?"

"Henry made like a ghost, he vaporized, but it was a magic trick."

Meeker thought back to the night she'd watched Reese die. He'd been above her, and when she'd heard the bullets, he'd fallen. She wanted to rush to him, but Becca pulled her away. As she replayed the scene in her mind, something came into clear focus. There was no blood. He'd been shot, but he hadn't bled out. She looked back at her sister.

"Why?" she demanded.

"Why what?"

"Why the lie?"

"It was the only way to be sure no one knew. He had to vaporize. It granted his wish to serve overseas."

"So it was all to get him behind the lines?"

"He was given an option," Alison explained, this time in normal English. "He made his decision on the plane over the Atlantic. He decided to share his skills with the underground. They needed a man who could do what he did."

Meeker thought back to the plane ride. Henry had opened his heart up to her, and she had rejected him. That must have pushed him to leave the team and his old life behind. And then he met Gail Worel. She found a way to somehow reconcile both service and love. She was willing to risk her heart even during a time of war. She had given Henry what Meeker could not.

"Helen."

Meeker waved her sister off. She had the story; in fact, she had written it with her own desire to be more than just a normal woman. Pushing out of the chair, she walked over to the window and looked out on the lawn. Folding her arms over her chest, she sadly shook her head. How many times had she prayed for a miracle? How many times had she dreamed Henry had somehow survived? Her prayers and dreams had been answered and somehow had turned into a nightmare.

"Is there anything I can say?" Alison asked.

"Are they happy?"

"Becca seems to think they are."

"And what's going to happen to them?"

"After they file reports and brief the President on something Henry uncovered that seems to be top secret, they're heading to the UK where he will go behind the lines and work once more with the underground."

Meeker nodded. "What's your word for someone who is dead?"

"Zombie?"

"Give me something else."

"A floater," Alison replied.

"That's what Henry is to me … a floater. If he stays dead, he can't hurt me."

"I understand. You are going to live a lie rather than face the truth."

Alison was on target, but it was far more complicated than that. In a weird twist, Meeker was again alive as was the man she thought she loved and while it should have changed everything, in reality, it didn't change anything. She and Henry still couldn't be together. She'd blown her chance to make that happen. So there was now no time for regrets, no time to mourn what could have been, only time to move on and do her best not to look back.

Meeker turned, "You have a file for me?"

"Yes, it's on the refinery explosions."

"Good, I need something to work on."

CHAPTER 17

Wednesday, July 28, 1942
4:13 p.m.
Grant Hotel, Chicago, Illinois

After checking into the Grant Hotel, Meeker tossed her notes on her bed and studied the scene outside her window. It seemed like only yesterday, she had been here with Reese working on that kidnapping case. When she had finally solved it, she had returned to this city to meet a sister she was sure was dead. This was also the place her tenure with the FBI had ended. Thus, Chicago held a lot of memories for Meeker, but for the moment, it was also a place to begin a new phase of her life.

The President wanted Meeker to look into the refinery fires that had been plaguing the nation for almost two months. The file she had been given wrote of destruction so great the cause of each explosion could not be pinpointed. Thus, the final verdicts for the five had been written off as accidental. The fact that more than three hundred men and women had lost their lives in the calamities led to newspapers demanding the industry take a look at both their hiring practices and the number of hours their employees worked each day. If there hadn't been a state of war, Congress might even have held committee meetings on this matter.

As she studied the reports on her train ride to Chicago, she found herself questioning the practice of working employees on twelve-hour shifts. This would seem to be a recipe for just the type of issues that had happened. But the nation's need for fuel meant that practice was likely not going to stop.

So what about the folks working in that industry? Were they qualified? The simple answer was no. Most of the experienced refinery workers were now in the military. Those filling their positions were either retired men coming back to work, those who physically couldn't qualify for service, or women. Many voices were now loudly blaming females for the disasters. Meeker dismissed that theory. So what did that leave?

For all the talk of politicians and the plots from a dozen movies, she had seen no evidence of any kind of organized underground group operating within US borders. Was that because the Nazis and Imperial Japan had not had the time to set up the network? If that was the case, perhaps these explosions were a sign the Axis powers were finally establishing such a ring, and these events were just signs of more things to come. While Meeker would, at least, consider the possibility, she still couldn't believe it. The reason for resistance to the idea went back to Fister.

Alistar Fister had not been an enemy agent. He had no passion for Nazi Germany; he was working to gain personal power. So who was pulling his strings and what did they want? If she could answer those questions, she felt she might be closer to knowing if the refinery explosions were planned or accidental.

Instincts suggested the tall man, the one she hadn't been able to identify and had only seen once, might have had something to do with this. She also sensed it was this mysterious man who had ordered Fister to eliminate her. But why? Was it for the Nazis or was it for something much more American—the lust for power and money?

From the sixteenth floor, Meeker thought about the case as she watched the busy traffic slowly making its way from corner to corner. The hurry up and wait mentality of the drivers was almost mesmerizing. Like rats in a maze, they were seemingly going nowhere but still couldn't give up trying to find a way to get ahead. She was so caught up in this vehicular ballet she almost didn't hear the ringing of the phone. Pulling herself from a trance, she crossed the room to a desk and picked up the receiver.

"Helen Meeker."

"Dizzy Vance."

"Ah, are you sure you should be calling me?"

"It's fine," he replied, "I'm still very much alive as far as the public is concerned, so no one connects me with anything other than bad suits, empty gin bottles, and sleazy comments."

She couldn't fault his logic or honesty. He was all that and more.

"I thought you gave up booze," she noted.

"I did, and I dress a lot better now too, but my dramatic upgrade in style is not the reason for this call. Rather it's my knowledge of Chicago, especially the city's underbelly.

So, the President felt I might be of some use to you on this caper."

"I can use the help," she admitted.

"Helen, I'm in the lobby. Do you want me to hang out down here, go to my room or come up to see you?"

"Why don't you come on up. I'm 1620."

As she waited for the private investigator, Meeker took off her hat, pushed her notes back into the file, switched on the radio and soon, the strains of "Jingle, Jangle, Jingle" by Kay Kaiser and His Band filled the room. She listened to the cowboy-themed tune about the joys of being single and considered the lyrics' sad irony. Only a knock halted her private pity party.

Vance was dressed in a smart, blue serge suit, his white shirt pressed and red tie perfectly knotted. As he removed his hat, Meeker noted the investigator's hair was clean and combed too. He had upgraded!

"It seems like it's been a long time," Vance noted as he strolled in.

"A different lifetime," she suggested as she closed the door.

The man walked over to the window, stuck his hands in his pocket and studied the same scene Meeker was noting when he had called. She allowed the big man to enjoy the view for about a minute before posing the question he surely knew was coming.

"What's your best guess?"

"From what I've studied," he announced, "It's no accident. Odds are too long for that."

"So," Meeker asked, "who's behind it?"

He turned and shrugged. After taking a seat in one of the room's two wooden chairs, he made an observation that had nothing to do with the case.

"Did you ever notice there are no thirteenth floors in most hotels? It just skips from twelve to fourteen. We claim to be civilized people who long ago escaped the superstitions of our ancestors and yet, we still secretly cling to the same fears. I'll fess up. I avoid stepping on cracks in the sidewalk like they could hurt me. Why is that?"

Meeker smiled. "Are you avoiding my question?"

"You have to ask yourself who had the most to gain? The answer seems obvious … the Nazis or Japs."

"But," Meeker argued, "do they have an organization in place that could pull something like this off?"

"And that's the problem," Vance replied. "I don't think they do. But who else benefits?"

"Dizzy, I've been asking myself that ever since I got on the train in Washington. I can point out the losers: the war effort, insurance companies, and the families of those who died in the explosions. But who really wins?"

"How about the plant owners?"

Meeker walked over to the other chair, opened her file, placed it on the desk and pulled out a legal pad covered with her notes. "Look at this. The refineries that have been hit are actually a bit underinsured. So the companies that own them are losing too."

"So it has to be the Germans," Vance suggested. "Nothing else makes any sense at all."

"Actually," Meeker suggested, "there's one more thing I've thought of. Let me ask you a question, who is going to win the war?"

"I think we are," the man quickly replied. "I'd put the odds four to one in our favor."

"Yeah," Meeker agreed, "we're behind right now, and it might take a year or two to catch up, but we have too many resources to be beaten. And, you add that neither one of our enemies have a viable chance at hitting us on our own shores works in our favor as well."

"Okay, Helen, we're on the same page in what we think will happen with the war. What does that have to do with your theory on who is behind this?"

Meeker picked up a pencil and tapped it on the table. "If we are going to win and that's something we can agree on, then the only thing left on the table is delaying that victory."

"What?"

"Who in this country benefits from our taking an extra year or so to win this war?"

A wide-eyed Vance rubbed his fleshy jaw before noting, "There are certain industries that would. I don't mean the big ones like Ford or General Motors, they will make huge profits when peace returns, but there are smaller ones whose owners are thriving only because they're producing things to fight the Germans and Japanese. Some of them were almost out of business when the Japanese bombed Hawaii and will likely be in trouble when this war ends."

"Now you're on my page," Meeker suggested. "I've uncovered other issues at plants where there have been slowdowns caused by unexplained equipment failure or delays in delivering materials. These issues might be tied into this same kind of thing. Now, beyond industry, who else?"

"Those behind the black market."

"Aren't there people in organized crime making more than they did in prohibition?" she asked.

Vance snapped his fingers, "Some are!"

"Okay," Meeker answered, "then I'll go to work on the industries that might benefit, and you starting digging into the black market. By the way, I'm going to tour the scene of the Illinois Pure Refinery explosion tomorrow, as well as visit with those who inspected that fire and probed for its cause. While I'm doing that, why don't you start using your old contacts with the police and the underworld and see if we can't find someone in the black market who is associated."

"I'll get on it," he announced as he got up and headed to the door. He was about to reach for the knob when her voice stopped him.

"Dizzy, did Henry seem happy when he was with Gail?"

The investigator uncomfortably shrugged. "I'm not good at reading those kind of things."

"Yes, you are," Meeker corrected him. "You read people like a book. Now be honest."

"He was happy."

"Good," she announced, her voice cracking a bit, "That's really good. I mean it. I'm glad they found each other. Everyone needs someone in times like this."

"Yes, ma'am," the man whispered as he opened the door and exited the room.

CHAPTER 18

Thursday, July 30, 1942
8:15 p.m.
Outside the Grant Hotel, Chicago, Illinois

It was hot, humid night as Dizzy Vance stepped out of the hotel and onto the sidewalk. The city's lights, somewhat muted because of the war's restriction on the use of power, bathed the street in a hazy glow that seemed as artificial as it really was. After the investigator glanced across the street to a clock hanging in a drug store window, he turned right and began the stroll toward Michigan Avenue. In thirty minutes, he would meet with Pugsy Weaver, a former boxer turned gopher for the O'Toole gang. Though his light often burned dim, likely due to the thousands of punches the man had blocked with his face, Weaver still was a good source. If he couldn't tell Vance about the local black market, the investigator was sure the small time hood would point him in the right direction.

Vance had walked a half block north when a small, dapperly dressed man stepped out of a taxi. And while he had aged, Vance still knew the face. In fact, though he had only seen it once, it was etched into even the deepest recesses of his mind with a clarity the best camera lens and film couldn't capture.

His blood at a boil, Vance stopped just behind as the man paid the cabbie, then as the man turned, the investigator jammed a pistol his ribs and whispered, "You walk with me, or you die right here. It's your choice."

"What's this all about?"

"Old, unsettled business," Vance explained. "Do you want to bleed all over this sidewalk or would you rather accompany me someplace where we can talk?"

"I'm a talker," came the quick reply.

Vance reached inside the man's silk jacket and retrieved a gun from a shoulder holster. After he'd dropped the weapon into his pocket, he asked, "Do I need to look for another?"

"You can, but you won't find anything."

"Okay, we're going to pretend to be old friends then. I'm keeping this gun aimed at your heart while we walk back to the Grant Hotel. Once we get through the lobby, up the elevator, and into my room, I'll give you both space and a chance to talk. You got that."

"Sure, I'll make like you're my long lost brother."

The stranger was true to his word. He tried nothing. It took four minutes get back to the hotel, waltz through the lobby and ride to the second floor. When the pair arrived at #2142, Vance handed his prisoner the key.

"Okay, open the door and move to the center of the room. Raise your hands as you walk."

"You're giving the orders," came the quick response.

The small man twisted the knob, lifted his arms and walked eight feet. As he did, Vance stepped inside, switched on the light, closed and locked the door. The stranger waited, hands held high until the investigator walked to a chair and sat down.

"You sit in the chair opposite me," Vance suggested.

Lowering his hands, the guest moved three paces to his right and eased down onto the wooden-backed chair. After crossing his arms over his chest, he posed a question. "Who are you working for? Which gang is it?"

Vance shook his head and grinned. "I'm dealing for Uncle Sam."

"Well, I'm 4-F, I've paid my taxes and my record is clean, so you really have no business with me."

"My business with you goes back a long way," Vance cracked.

"Have we met?"

"Yeah, on a rural road, I was an off-duty cop, and I happened upon you when you had car trouble on the day you and your friend had robbed a bank."

The visitor slowly nodded. "Your kid was shot. And then the guy I was with took your wife and your car. I read later the kid died. I'm sorry about that."

"You sorry about executing my wife?" the investigator spat.

"Yeah, the thought of your wife being shot like that still haunts me. I can also still see the look on your kid's face when the bullet hit. I can't erase either from my mind."

"Neither can I," Vance whispered.

"In case you're wondering, my name is Stanford Poole. My friends call me Stan."

"I'm not your friend. But Stan, I've only got one question for you. Why did you have to kill my wife?"

"You won't believe it," Poole announced, his voice steady and sure, "but I recently had this same conversation with Big Jim O'Toole."

"Did you tell him how much fun it was?" Vance hissed. "Did you brag about the way she screamed and begged for her life?"

"No, I informed him that if I hadn't been at the wrong place at the wrong time, I would likely be a college professor now."

"That's a really good story," Vance cut in, "maybe you should sell it to one of the pulps."

"Here is the rest of it. I was on a college break when a friend convinced me to take a ride with him. I didn't know he was going to rob a bank. Then you ran into us."

"And I saw your face," Vance noted as he waved his gun, "and knew I'd never forget it. And, when I met you again someday, I'd make you beg, then I'd beat on you some and finally murder you one piece at a time. I've been waiting a long time to fulfill that promise."

"She didn't beg," Poole matter-of-factly explained.

"What?"

"Your wife, she didn't beg. She displayed more courage than anyone I've ever known."

"So you killed her?"

"No, I didn't," Poole replied, "you won't believe it, but I begged my old high school friend to let her go. He told me he couldn't do that. When I tried to stop him, he clubbed me with the butt of his gun. I was just getting to my feet when he shot her. And I've been trapped in this sordid world ever since."

"You're quite a storyteller; maybe you should move to Hollywood."

Poole grimly shook his head. "You don't move away from Jim O'Toole. By the way, you know mine, so what's your name? I'd kind of like to know who was signing my death certificate."

"Dizzy Vance."

"I like it. There's something about having someone named Dizzy punch my ticket that's satisfying." He paused and shook his head. "Do I have time to share a story before you show me the grand exit?"

"If it's short."

"I'll make it short," Poole assured Vance. "The guy who drilled your wife became a hit man. He was a sick puppy. He took pleasure in pain. He worked for O'Toole until he overstepped even Big Jim's rather loose rules."

"What did he do?" Vance demanded.

"He tried to make money by horning in on a kidnapping. He found out about the deal, plugged the guy who did the deed and then tried to cash in on his own."

"So, O'Toole draws the line at kidnapping?"

"No," Poole admitted, "but he doesn't kidnap someone who's crippled. This young woman was a polio victim. O'Toole's sister was hit with the disease, so he has soft spot for kids who have to deal with infantile paralysis."

Suddenly Vance's mind went back to the night in the Eastside Motor Court in Gary, Indiana. Sure he was older, a lot rougher looking, but he had seen the kidnapper before. When the investigator held his fire that night, his wife's killer walked out that door.

"What's wrong, you look like you've seen a ghost."

"If this happened a couple of months back, I was the man that rescued the young woman. If that is the case, I can't believe I let him walk."

"Small world," Poole finally mused after both men spent a silent two minutes considering what Vance had just discovered. "Who was really behind that deal before Gus horned in on it? It wasn't anyone local, O'Toole checked on that."

"You wouldn't believe me if I told you," Vance shot back. He studied the visitor's eyes for a few seconds and then posed another question. "Have you been straight with me?"

"Yeah. I've got nothing to gain by lying."

"Why should I believe a hit man?"

"I stop gang murders," Poole explained, "I don't commit them. I'm the guy who oversees operations and manages action. O'Toole trusts me to delegate the work and make sure the books all balance. In the world of crime, I'm the white collar guy."

"So you want me to believe you've never killed anyone?"

"The word on the street is I have a lot of notches," Poole admitted, "but that's simply to make sure no one tries to rub me out. In truth, I've only murdered one person in cold blood. And I've never lost a bit of sleep over that job."

"Can you get me to Gus?" Vance asked.

"Sure, I can give you the address. I could even take you there, but not sure how much satisfaction you'd get from it."

"If you were me," the investigator asked, "wouldn't you want to take care of it? Wouldn't you want to plug the guy who killed your wife in cold blood?"

"Yeah, I would. There's no doubt in my mind that few things would give me greater satisfaction."

Vance mulled over Poole's offer for a few seconds before standing, retrieving a pad and pencil and tossing it toward his guest. "Write down the address."

Poole quickly jotted down the information and tossed it back to the investigator. "I gave you the directions from here as well. But could I make a suggestion? Call it granting me a final wish if you will."

"What?"

"Don't go until tomorrow morning. I suggest between seven and nine. Besides, tonight you will need to dispose of my body, and that will take some time."

Vance slipped his gun back into pocket and shook his head. "If I let you fly are you going to warn Gus I'm on the way?"

"No," Poole assured him, "nor am I going to tell O'Toole we met. I think I'd rather just keep this between us. But why not shoot me?"

"That day I came upon you two working on the car is as vivid now as if it happened this afternoon. I can still see everything. I remember you down to the color of your eyes and the dirt on your shirtsleeves. Now, I understand something else too. The look your face was one mixed with horror and fear. And you didn't shoot—you froze. I don't know why I didn't get that before. And there was a knot on your forehead that looked like you'd been hit by the gun butt."

"You lost your wife and child," Poole said, "and that loss will haunt me until I die. I am very sorry. I really am."

Vance nodded. "Can I ask you something else?"

"Even if you're not pointing it at me, you're still the man with the gun."

"Is O'Toole involved in the black market?"

"Carfono was, O'Toole's not. He might well be an immoral crime boss, but he's at least patriotic unless you count paying taxes. He draws the line there. He doesn't see taxes as a part of patriotism. Are you investigating the black market? In Chicago, those who run it are mostly small time operators filling different specialized segments of the market."

"What about the refinery explosions?" the investigator quizzed. "Are we dealing with anything relating to the underworld?"

"Not that I know of," Poole assured him. "I can tell you this; on the West Coast, there are some elements of organized crime that are heavily involved in that business. So blowing one up here might well pump up their profits."

"Can you give me names?"

"Mr. Vance, I think you know them."

Vance paused, ran his hand over his jaw and nodded. "Poole, are you sure I need to wait until tomorrow morning to take Gus?"

"It will be better for you if you do," the visitor assured him. "Also, you might need a night to really take stock of your actions. Now, if I come upon any information you need on the refinery, how do I get ahold of you?"

"Seriously? You would share information?"

"All of us are looking for a way out," Poole admitted. "Maybe you could help me find a place where no one would know who I was. I'd love try to start over again. After all, I've only killed one man, and I'd like to find a way to not add to that total."

Vance reached into his pocket and scribbled down a number. "It's reversed so no one else would be able to figure it out. You will be able to talk to whoever answers. But they won't make a deal without you supplying real information."

Poole stood and took the paper. After reading it once, he wadded it up and tossed in on the table. Noted the confused look on Vance's face, he explained. "Photographic memory. Not having paper trails serves me well. Am I free to go?"

"Yeah."

"Sure you don't want to kill me?"

"For the moment, I am. But you don't get your gun back until I go face to face with Gus."

"I understand," Poole smiled as he moved to the door, unlocked it and walked out into the hall.

Vance watched until the man stepped onto the elevator then closed the door and walked over to the window. There was no reason to visit with Pugsy now. Poole had given him the information that removed organized crime from the mix. Tomorrow, if he survived a morning appointment, he would check on his sources to see if some small time hoods were trying to move their game up a notch or two. Now, it was time to clean his gun and get a good night's sleep.

CHAPTER 19

Friday, July 31, 1942
7:15 a.m.
3800 North Narragansett Avenue, Chicago, Illinois

It was a determined Dizzy Vance who walked out of the Grant Hotel and waved for a cab. After a night of little sleep, he'd risen early, eaten a big breakfast, had a professional shave, taken a shower and dressed in a navy pinstripe suit, light blue shirt and red and white striped tie. After getting his shoes polished and tossing the boy a dollar tip, he'd gone back to his room, retrieved both his gun and Stanford Poole's Smith and Wesson and taken the stairs to the lobby. Once there, he left a note explaining his situation and had the desk clerk put it in Helen Meeker's box. That way, if he didn't come back, she would know his death had nothing to do with their current case.

A red and yellow Chevy sedan, now serving duty as a taxi, pulled up to the curb. Opening the back door, Vance slipped in and fell back into the seat.

"It's a beautiful day," the driver called out.

"Yeah, I guess it is," the investigator mumbled.

The man behind the wheel looked to be about sixty-five, with close-cropped salt and pepper hair, dark eyes and olive skin. His family roots likely could be traced back to Italy or Greece. His medium build and well-defined shoulders pointed to his being a part of some type of manual labor before falling into the world of moving people from place to place.

"Where to?" the cabbie asked.

The address had been on his mind all night. This was the place either he or the man who killed his wife was going to breathe their final breath. He would either be the judge, jury, and executioner, or he would end his life right here in the city where he used to work.

"I need to go to 3800 North Narragansett Avenue, #342 A."

"I can get to you the address," the cabbie announced, "but you'll have to find the number yourself."

"That's fine?"

"You visiting someone there?" the driver asked as he pulled out into traffic.

"Yeah."

"A family member?"

"No, just someone I've been looking to find for a very long time."

"Got it."

On the drive over the cabbie, who informed Vance his name was Geppie, talked about everything from the war to the White Sox. The investigator heard little the driver said. His mind was focused his mission, and so, he was trying to anticipate every possible scenario that might play out.

The address seemed to indicate he lived in an apartment. That was better than a house as there were fewer exits. If Poole had been straight with him, then Gus would be alone. That meant he likely wouldn't be expecting company with firepower. As early as it was, he might even be asleep.

With traffic, the drive took more than half an hour, and the cab passed through a half a dozen different interesting neighborhoods, each one echoing the birth country of its founders. The cab also motored by two large cemeteries. When the taxi passed by an almost castle-like structure with an interesting looking front gate, the driver did a U-turn and parked.

"We are here," Geppie announced. "Do you want me to wait?"

"No," Vance replied. "What do I owe you?"

"It's not cheap to come this far, the meter says three and a quarter."

The investigator reached into his inside coat pocket and pulled out a five. Pushing the bill toward the driver, he announced, "Keep the change."

"Thank you, and I hope the visit brings you a sense of peace."

Vance shrugged as he got out of the cab and watched it drive away. Fingering his gun, but keeping it in his pocket, he took a deep breath and walked across the street to the stone castle. As he approached the open gate, he froze. Chiseled into the archway was Mt. Olive Cemetery. Moving his eyes to the left, he checked the address—3800 North Narragansett Avenue. The sign assured him he was in the right place. So, what was this all about? Then it dawned on him, Poole had sold him a bill of goods. He'd been conned from the get-go. How could he fall for something like that? Suddenly filled with rage, a red-faced Vance marched over to a uniformed guard at the gate and hissed, "How can I get a cab?"

"I can call you one," the man assured him, "but you just got here."

"I'm the victim of a bad joke … a very bad joke. A man gave me this address and told me I could find who I wanted at #342 A."

"That's funny," the guard announced, "you're the second guy who's been here today looking for that number. Is your name Vance?"

"Yeah," the now confused investigator admitted.

"Well, a guy named Poole came by an hour ago. He asked me how to find a grave and then he left a few things there. He gave me your name and told me you'd pick them up. Do you still want me to call that cab or should I show you the way to the grave?"

Still confounded by the situation, Vance looked through the gates and them back to the guard before announcing, "Lead the way."

For several minutes, the two walked around gravestones, by monuments and over gravel lanes. Finally, on a small hill at the end of the cemetery, they came upon a fairly fresh grave. The dirt was still in a mound, and there was no marker. Beside the grave was a large, sealed cardboard box with an envelope attached.

"You know who's buried here?" Vance asked, his eyes seemingly trying to look through the dirt.

"A middle-aged guy named Augustus Prime. At least, that's what they said his name was. The man at the funeral home told me that he had several others. Not surprising as he was a hood."

"How did he die?" Vance asked.

"You can look it up in the newspapers, but I'll save you the trouble; he was gunned down by parties unknown. In other words, the cops have no leads. And as this probably involved one hood taking out another, Prime's murder is not going to ever be high on the police 'to do' list."

The investigator leaned over and picked up the box. Taking the envelope off, he handed the package to the guard. "Would you hold this for a minute?"

As the man looked on, Vance tore open the eight-by-ten-inch envelope. Reaching inside, he found a smaller, sealed envelope and several photos. Pushing the smaller envelope into his inside coat pocket, Vance turned his attention to the pictures. The first one appeared to have been cut out of a high school yearbook. This image clearly showed the man he had confronted so long ago. The other four were obviously the same person as he aged.

"Is this the guy who was buried in this grave?" the investigator asked as showed the pictures to the guard.

"Yes, I can assure you it is. As the man had no family and friends at the service, the staff served as pallbearers. We decided to open up the lid and take a look at the body. You don't get many chances to see a guy who has been rubbed out. I'm never doing that again. What we saw wasn't pretty, but that scar on his forehead matches up. So it's the same guy."

Vance took a final look at the grave, stuffed the photos into the envelope, grabbed the box and began his trek to the front gate. He said nothing to the guard until the man had made the call to order a taxi. As the car drove up, the investigator offered, "I thank you for your time."

"You're welcome, sir."

The cab ride back was made in twenty-five minutes. It took just four more for Vance to get to his room. Once there, he locked the door and took the box to the table. Pulling out a pocket knife, he cut the twine and opened the cardboard folds. Inside, he found stacks of money along with a snub-nosed thirty-eight. He studied the contents for a few seconds before reaching into his pocket and retrieving the letter. Moving to a chair, he sat down and torn it open.

> *Vance,*
>
> *You will find most of the money that Gus got from the kidnapping. If the police kept the bullets, the gun can be used to tie him to at least a dozen murders. It was also the gun he used to shoot your wife.*
>
> *By now, you likely realize that when I confessed to murdering only one man in my life, I was talking about Gus. And it was murder too. He was unarmed when I gunned him down. And I don't feel guilty.*
>
> *I'll be in touch.*
>
> *Sincerely,*
>
> *Stanford Poole*

Vance stood, placed the letter on top of the gun and walked to the window. He was numb and empty. He also felt cheated. He should have been the one to dispatch Gus.

After all, that one goal had shaped his life for years. Now the book had been closed without his writing the final chapter. Perhaps it was better this way. Rather than having a man who now worked for the President sink to the level of a hate-fueled hood, the gun had been fired by a man who was employed by Big Jim O'Toole.

As he watched the traffic stream by, as he listened to blasting horns and people's shouts, he thought back to the man who had penned the ending. Just like Vance, Poole's life had been forever altered on that day when they first came face to face. While he didn't lose his family, he did lose his future.

THE 13TH FLOOR

CHAPTER 20

Friday, July 31, 1942
12:17 p.m.
Ruins of the refinery, Chicago, Illinois

What was left of the refinery was located twenty miles north of Chicago on the shores of Lake Michigan. Much like the arson squad that had been there when the embers were still warm, the visitor saw nothing that could help her define if this was another bizarre accident or sabotage. As she sat across the desk from the facility's owner, she posed the question he no doubt had expected since learning of her visit.

"Do you think this was an accident?"

Joseph Jacoby, J. J. to his friends, was about five-eight, perhaps one hundred-forty pounds, with thin lips, deep-set brown eyes, and a head full of dark hair. Dressed in a well-fitted suit with a shirt and no tie, his face reflected his lack of sleep. The dark circles under his eyes almost reached to his mouth. He appeared to be a man completely consumed by grief while also drowning in despair. Leaning back in his chair, he looked out the second-floor window toward where his plant had once stood.

"Miss Meeker," he began, "I had been making personal inspections for two weeks before the explosion. I'd spent hours in the plant each day studying my workers for signs of fatigue. My foremen had been stressing safety, and we were even taking extra breaks each day. The night of the explosion, my personal physician was in the plant checking out each one on the shift. He was there when the blast hit. We still haven't found his body."

"So," Meeker suggested, "your answer is no."

He turned his eyes back to his guest and shook his head. "There have been too many of them."

"Too many of what?" she asked.

"Too many unexplained refinery explosions. I was, therefore, doing everything I could prevent that from happening here."

Jacoby was a man clearly shaken and obviously cared a great deal about his employees. Still, she had to get this one point cleared before she could move forward.

"Mr. Jacoby, pardon me for asking, but did you have your plant sufficiently insured?"

He nodded. "I know what you're driving at; the local investigators asked the same thing. I can tell you that I can rebuild the facility, but I'll have to reach into my private account to buy some of the equipment. So, I likely should have increased my coverage and failed to do so."

"I'm sorry."

Jacoby frowned, stood and walked over to the window. "Come over here, Miss Meeker." When she joined the refinery owner, he continued. "What do you see out there?"

She studied the twisted metal, jumbled piles of debris and a crumpled truck. As she looked at the mess, she began to sense she was viewing more than a wrecked refinery, she was looking at a man's dreams turned into a nightmare.

"I see what you have lost," Meeker noted.

"Actually," Jacoby sadly observed, "you don't. You see the physical damage, but I see the ghosts. I see old Roy Robbins, who worked with me for twenty years. He left a wife, three grown sons, and five grandkids. I also see Joyce Carlton. Her husband is in the Navy stationed in the Pacific, she has a year-old daughter, and she had been working here for three days. I see Martha Rison, a woman who once ran a daycare, raised a couple of her own kids, and was the sponsor of a Girl Scout troop." He turned to face his guest. "I see everyone who worked in that plant. I see them when I look out that window, when I drive my car, when I eat my supper and when I try to sleep."

Jacoby closed his eyes as tears ran down his face. Trying to regain his composure, he whispered, "I lost my wife five years ago. We never had kids. Those people who died in that explosion were my family. It's not the building, it is not the refinery though we do need both for the war effort, it is all about the people. You need to understand that."

Meeker nodded. Though she couldn't feel it like he did, she could understand. She felt that way when Henry—but he didn't really die. Suddenly, she was consumed with anger. She had mourned Henry's death. She had been consumed by guilt. She had blamed herself for everything. There was not a night that her sleep had not been haunted by nightmares. How many times had she seen him die? How many times had she woken up screaming? How many times had she questioned her own value as a person and a leader?

"Miss Meeker?"

Shaking her head as if that would toss out the emotions ripping through her mind and heart, she looked at her host but said nothing.

"You do understand?" Jacoby asked.

"No," Meeker finally admitted, "I've lost people I love, but not like you have. My ghosts are far fewer."

Looking into her eyes, the small man with the huge heart frowned. "Who did this to my plant?"

Meeker shrugged. "I don't know yet, but the President has assigned me to find it out."

"Why just you?" Jacoby wondered. "Why not hundreds?"

"If you want the truth," Meeker explained, "it's because the FBI just views this as an accident. As the arson squads have come up with nothing that points to sabotage, Hoover has decided the explosions were caused by fatigue or having inexperienced people in key positions."

"But I looked into that," he argued. "I was in my plant every day and night. I had my people checked out. It has to be something else. I don't want those who died here to have a legacy of causing this. That's not how I want them remembered. And I don't want to be known as the man who worked his people to their deaths. Those things are all lies!"

"I'll guarantee we'll find the answers," Meeker assured him. "On the train ride here, I looked at reports on each of your employees. I studied their backgrounds. I tried to find something suspicious that might indicate they would be plants or a mole. The President also pulled three Secret Service agents and four members of his personal staff to look at the background of everyone who worked at the other plants. On the basis of what we could find, there were only two people who were suspicious. One of them worked in Houston and the other in San Diego. Interviews by field agents assured us they were not involved in any kind of sabotage."

"I guess that's something," Jacoby sadly noted.

"That's not all," Meeker continued. "As you've probably realized, none of the explosions have taken place at a facility run by one of our large oil companies. Over the past twenty-four hours, I have also looked at each of the owners of these plants. I have made calls, studied insurance policies and dug much deeper than the FBI did. None of them had a single reason to blow up their own facilities."

"So you know nothing."

"Oh, no," Meeker argued. She looked back to the scene of the disaster before continuing. "I actually know who is not responsible, and that's something. And, unlike much of the press and many in Congress, I don't think this is caused by fatigue or having the wrong people in the wrong positions."

"Then what?" Jacoby demanded. "Who killed my people?"

"What's interesting to me," Meeker noted, "is that there is not a real pattern to the explosions. Some of the plants were refining gasoline, others aircraft fuel and still others diesel. So what is being produced has nothing to do with the explosions."

"It still sounds like you know nothing," he argued, frustration obvious in his tone.

"Use logic," the visitor suggested. "The owners aren't involved, the employees are not involved and the product being produced is not the cause. So that leaves us with one question … who benefits when these independent facilities are not in operation?"

"Who?" he demanded.

"How about the big companies? More of the production falls to them. And don't kid yourself, there is a lot profit made by businesses during war."

"I don't see it," Jacoby argued. "They just don't have the capacity. I lean toward Nazi agents."

"But," Meeker pointed out, "I don't think they have the organization on the ground to do that kind of work. Maybe they could knock out one plant, but not five."

"Someone is behind it," the facility's owner moaned, "and that means someone murdered June, Doris, Tom, Rachel, Jim, Diane …"

As the man continued to name his employees, Meeker was struck by something she had missed. It was so obvious too.

Quickly moving back to chair where she'd been sitting, she grabbed her purse. As a curious Jacoby looked on, Meeker made a request. "I need to make a call. And I need privacy. Can I use your phone, and can you leave me alone in your office?"

"Sure."

She watched the man exit and close the door before she took the receiver and dialed zero. When the operator picked up, she asked for long distance. Three minutes later the line at the Washington office of the FBI rang. She went through the switchboard before being connected to the unlikely person she was determined to reach.

"Hello."

"Teresa Bryant."

"Yes."

"This is Helen Meeker. I'm calling from Chicago. I need your help."

"My help?"

"Yes, I just remembered a quote and I need for you to employ your special skills to dig into the man behind those words."

"My special skills?"

"Seduction," Meeker explained, "so if you're game, you'll be needing that dress you wore to my room the other night. Or at least, one like it. Are you interested?"

Bryant kept Meeker hanging for at least thirty seconds. Finally, just when Meeker believed she had lost the connection, a voice came back on the line.

"Who is the target?"

"Senator Jeb North."

"He's a wolf," Bryant cracked. "He was studying my every move at the Root's last weekend."

"Then the ground work has been completed," Meeker noted.

"I'm not concerned about the ground work," Bryant explained, "He has other things in mind. But why do you need information from him?"

"Can you get me his real view on women? And can you dig up his connections to big business ... especially anything connected to the war industry?"

"Well," Bryant replied, "he will be at the party Mrs. Root has me attending tomorrow night. So, I might as well saddle up to him and do a bit of digging. But what's the objective? You owe me that much."

"In truth, I'm at a dead end on a matter I'm handling for the President. I think North's rhetoric might be inciting someone to blow up refineries. I would like to know more about what he really thinks about women. In the meantime, I'm going to look into people and groups who might be influenced by North's words."

"Sounds like you're playing a long shot to me."

"In this case," Meeker explained, "I've exhausted everything else."

"Helen, can I ask one more thing?"

"Sure."

"Why call me?"

"You saved my life."

"Don't put too much stock in that," Bryant warned, "I was only there to give you a file on a man I wanted to bring down. I wasn't there for any other reason."

Meeker carefully considered the explanation before noting, "Then let's say I'm playing another long shot. You know where I'm staying in Washington. I'll be back there tomorrow. Call me if you get anything you feel you have something that might help in this matter."

"Okay."

As the line went dead, Meeker grabbed her purse and hurried out the door. If her hunch was right, there was a lot of work to be done. If she was wrong, then she had no idea where to look next.

CHAPTER 21

Saturday, August 1, 1942
9:05 p.m.
Home of General Jefferson Root, Washington, DC

Because she felt she needed to make a grand entrance, Teresa Bryant arrived at the party over an hour late. Wearing a red, off-the-shoulder dress that fit her form like a glove, the raven-haired beauty glided across the floor with the grace of a ballerina. As she eased into a Victorian chair in the far back of the cavernous room, four men rushed to her side to inquire if she needed a drink. In her first five minutes, she flirted with a general, two congressmen, and an ambassador, yet, during each of those playful conversations her dark eyes always managed to catch Jeb North's as the senator played billiards with Jefferson Root. The casual long distance interplay went on for almost an hour before the forty-five-year-old, tall, attractive North finally waltzed over to Bryant's side.

"I don't believe we have been formally introduced," he noted.

"Actually," she replied, "we shared a few moments at Mrs. Root's last party. I remember your blue eyes seemingly caressing me as I danced with Senator James."

"Was I being too forward?" he quipped.

Bryant ran a polished nail over her lips and smiled. "A woman likes to be noticed, especially by a handsome man."

"There are several men in this room much better looking than I am," he noted as he leaned closer. "But, do I love that perfume."

"It called Sin," she softly replied, "and the measure of a man is more than the way his face looks, it's the way he carries himself and the manner in which he speaks."

"And," North added, "how much power he wields and how much money he has in his bank account."

"Let's call those fashion accessories," Bryant suggested.

She took her eyes from North and studied the scene playing out before her. The lavishly decorated forty-by-forty-foot room served as the backdrop for both temptation and intrigue. A dozen of the most powerful men in the city, all dressed in formal jackets, were visiting with women Gertrude Root had hired to decorate the festivities. From time to time, two or three men would meet in quiet corners and, as they drank the finest liquor and smoked Cuban cigars, they pretended to determine the fate of the world. Or perhaps in front of the hundred-year-old tapestries and imported furniture, they actually were putting together deals that would shift power from one place to another. The future of the world had been cast in stranger places than this.

North leaned close and whispered, "More things are decided here than in Congress. You should be honored to be watching this. Soak it in."

She glanced up from the chair, her eyes catching his. He was looking at her as if she the top prize at the county fair. His almost arrogant expression indicated he felt he had already won it too.

"Have you seen the view from the terrace?" he asked.

"Should I?" she teased.

"I think you would enjoy it," North assured her.

"But, should you leave the deal makers?" she asked.

"They don't make their deals without me," he bragged. "So they will still be here when we return."

Bryant had done her homework on North. He was married but had no children. He had met his wife, Anna, in college, but she stayed home when he was in the capitol. This allowed him to be free to play the field without consequences. The press knew about North's dalliances, but as was the custom in Washington, no one reported them. Beyond his personal life, North was a politician whose wealth had grown immensely during his two terms as senator. He was not only a deal maker; he was also an opportunist. When he saw a hot issue, he determined the public's mood and jumped on it. Thus, when he realized a majority in the country had strong, emotional feelings on integration and immigration, he had echoed those thoughts in carefully constructed but fiery speeches. Did he believe what he said? Even those close to him had no idea.

"Miss ..."

"Bryant," she answered with a bat of her long dark lashes, "but you can call me Teresa. And yes, I'd love to see the terrace."

With fluidity usually only seen on the stage, Bryant uncrossed her legs and stood in one, flowing movement. Taking the hand offered to her, she then elegantly moved across the room, out the hall, and through the double French doors. North only released his grip long enough to shut the entry thus guaranteeing privacy.

"A woman should be judged by her beauty," he proposed as he followed her over to a three-foot-high stone wall separating the patio from the garden. "It's a shame we don't have a full moon; if we did, I'm sure your skin would literally glow."

North wasn't wasting any time. If she didn't slow his train down quickly, she might be taking a trip that was much longer than she was prepared to take.

"Why me?" she asked.

"You're the most beautiful woman here. And I worship beauty."

"You really don't know anything about me," Bryant pointed out.

"I can quickly solve that," he announced as he moved behind her and wrapped his arms around her waist. "Where are you from?"

"Several places," she answered as he pulled her against his body.

"Such as?"

"Arkansas, Oklahoma, and Louisiana to name three."

"So a woman from the south. I love the culture there. Those are places that still reflect American values."

"What values?" Bryant asked.

"In this city and others, the war has messed up the natural order of life. Women are working now. They are filling spots usually reserved for men."

"And that's bad?" she asked as North eased his chin against her bare neck.

"Teresa, what do you do?"

"I'm a secretary at the FBI."

"That's fine. That's a good place for a woman."

He was now too close, his hands inching toward places they didn't belong; she was going to have to make a move soon, but for the moment she didn't need to do anything that would change the subject. So, she tried to direct the conversation in a place she needed for it go.

"Senator, are there bad places for women?"

He allowed his lips to graze her neck before answering. "A woman's place is in the home. A single woman can be a nurse, maid, secretary or the like, but women are not suited for management or working in factories. God made this a man's world; we take the risks, do the hard labor and the women support us."

Taking a deep breath, Bryant turned and faced the senator. As she moved, his clutch grew even tighter. He was leaning forward to kiss her when she offered an observation.

"I have Indian in my blood. There was a Caddo woman who guided many men through early America. She did not stay home; she was a leader."

North gently shook his head and brought his index finger to her lips. "This is a place where European traditions reign."

"Why is it so wrong for a woman to push beyond normal expectations?" she gently demanded.

Her question seemed to catch him off guard. He released his arms and stepped back to restudy the woman whose charms he obviously wanted to share.

"In a word," North announced, "if women become involved in every facet of the workforce, if they begin to run companies or are elected to office, it will lead to the downfall of the American system. A man can handle a number of different things at the same time. We are jugglers by nature. A woman is by nature singularly focused. If she gains power, she will ignore her natural responsibilities as a wife and mother and then the entire moral system of this nation will break down."

"Do you believe that?" Bryant asked.

"Imagine men attempting to work alongside beautiful women. It would steal their focus. Our industrial machine would fall apart. I honestly believe the use of women in the workforce is a much more serious threat to the United States than Imperial Japan or Nazi Germany. Consider this, will a woman who tastes the power of being treated as an equal ever be satisfied going back to the way it was before the war? There is no better example than Helen Meeker. Here is a woman who is doing the work of a man. She has no time for love and no respect for men. Imagine ten million like her or fifty million. Meeker needs to be exposed and stopped before young women in this nation begin to dream of following in her footsteps."

"Senator," Bryant countered, "I've been told you're a smart politician who usually goes the direction the wind blows. But in this case, you sound as if your position is based on personal conviction."

"It is," he assured her. "I'll do anything it takes to save this country from complete moral decay."

"Would you mind explaining what kind of morals you are talking about?" she cooed.

North once more studied Bryant from the top of her head to her red pumps. When his eyes once more found hers, he explained, "I think it's a man's job to worship a woman and a woman's job to please a man. That enhances the fabric of the American society rather than tear it down."

He again closed the distance between them and swept her up in his arms. Though she didn't want to, she allowed him a kiss.

"Why don't we go back to my place," he suggested.

"Not tonight," she whispered. "I'm still an old-fashioned girl even if I don't dress like one."

"Too bad," he cracked, "but would you consider making a trip to Pennsylvania with me tomorrow? There's a man I need to meet there. We could spend the night and get to know each other better. I could call J. Edgar, and I'm sure he would give you a hall pass."

Bryant eased out of his arms and walked slowly toward the French doors leading back into the home. As she reached for the knob, she turned, slowly allowing her eyes to close and open, and asked, "What time do you need to leave?"

"About noon. Where do I pick you up?"

"I'm not ready to give you my address, so why not in front of the Washington Arms. I'll be there at fifteen after twelve."

Unsure of what she had gotten herself into, Bryant opened the door and returned to the party. A few minutes later, North entered and returned to the billiard table. Neither of them acknowledged the other for the remainder of the night.

THE 13TH FLOOR

CHAPTER 22

Saturday, August 1, 1942
11:05 p.m.
Grant Hotel, Washington, DC

Helen Meeker, dressed in satin pajamas with her hair pulled back in a ponytail, sat in the middle of her bed and looked at the hundreds of documents and notes spilled out in front of her. By now she had studied the files from every possible angle, so she felt she knew every detail of the owners' lives as well as their company's financial records for the past decade. She was also familiar with each plant worker that had been killed as well as those who had somehow escaped death. Once she had completed her study of the five facilities decimated by the explosions, she turned her attention the other independent refiners across the nation. She had already reviewed ownership, production and the age and size of the plants, and was breaking down each company's current workforce by both age and sex.

After taking a sip of Coke from a six-ounce bottle and nibbling on a Snickers candy bar, she looked at the chart she had created on a legal pad. Doing some quick math, she figured percentages, then got up and took those numbers across the room to an unfolded US map on a table. She had already circled the location of the refinery fires with a red pen. She had then circled the independent refineries that had not been hit in blue. Now grabbing a black pen, she looked at her math and began to scribble numbers beside those black circles. The first number identified the number of female employees at each facility. The next cited the percentage of the workforce that was women. After she had entered the last pair of numbers, she smiled and tapped the state of Pennsylvania with her pen.

Getting up, she took another sip of Coke and moved back to the bed. She crossed her legs Indian-style and pulled out a road atlas. Turning to Pennsylvania, she studied the northeastern part of the state and then traced a route back to Washington, DC. Was this too obvious? Was she fooling herself into believing she had an answer? The only way to find out was to make a trip. If her hunch was right, she was going save some lives. But there was still a glaring problem. Even if she knew the *where* and perhaps the *why*, she still had no idea as to the *who*. Until she knew "the who" behind this, the danger would continue. She had to stop this person or group before they figured out she could predict what refinery they would strike next. If they found out she could forecast their moves, they would surely change the targets and hit a different war-related industry.

The room's phone ringing pulled her eyes from the map. After glancing at her watch, she rolled over toward the nightstand and answered.

"Helen."

"I saw a photo in the *Times* today of you signing autographs. You are quite the celebrity."

"Is this Teresa?" Meeker asked.

"It is," came the quick reply.

"I don't want to be a celebrity. Being known in public makes my life very difficult. I'll be so glad when the press moves on."

"So what other perks of stardom have fallen in your lap?" Bryant inquired.

"You really want to know?"

"Yeah."

"I've been offered the chance to endorse clothing, hats, shoes, cosmetics, candy, soft drinks, and even shampoo. Two different magazines want me to write features, and a movie studio wants me to play myself in a story about my life."

"You will make a million," Bryant noted.

"I turned them all down. I don't want to make a million, I want to solve this case."

"Well, I have some good news for you," Bryant paused, "at least, I think it might be good. Jeb North does actually have a firm position on one issue."

"And that is?"

"He believes the most dangerous enemy to the American way of life is having women in the workforce. It was ironic, as, at the same time he was explaining how this would lead to the moral decay of the nation, he was trying to charm me into going back to his place."

"You predicted he was a wolf."

"Yeah. Now, Helen, what was so important about knowing if he believed the stuff he's been selling to the press about women?"

"I can't tell much more than I did last time," Meeker explained, "and that's due to the President's request for secrecy in this matter. But coupled with what I've found out today, let's just say that the man's rhetoric is likely inspiring a movement that has the same goal as North does."

"And that somehow leads to blowing up refineries?" Bryant asked.

"Yes. I'm going to make a trip to the one I think will be hit next to see if they'll increase security."

"I'm making a trip tomorrow as well. North asked me to accompany him to Pennsylvania."

"Where?" a suddenly very interested Meeker asked.

"I don't know the specific location, but I believe he's using my presence to continue a romantic attack he started tonight."

"How are you going to fight him off? Or are you?"

"He won't be scoring any points with me, I can make sure of that, but I do want to find out what the meeting he's scheduled—which is the supposed reason for the trip—is all about it. J. Edgar would love to have some dirt on the man, and I would like to be the one to deliver it. Do you need anything else?"

"No, I appreciate what you've done. If you do find anything specific that fits into what I'm working on, would you let me know?"

"Are we becoming friends?" Bryant asked.

"I don't trust you enough for that," Meeker admitted.

"So you're using me?"

"Yes, I am. I have no problem admitting that."

"Okay, as long as I know the score. But realize, I will likely be using you someday too."

"I know I'm getting into debt," Meeker acknowledged. "Be careful on the trip."

"I can take care of myself."

Meeker laughed, "I have no doubt about that."

As the line went dead, Meeker laid her head on the pillow. Why was Jeb North taking Bryant to Pennsylvania?

Picking up her legal pad she scribbled a note reminding her to get the make, model and license number of the car or cars the senator used. If she and North ended up in the same location, she wanted to know about it. Now, it was time to uncover her bed and try to get some sleep.

CHAPTER 23

Sunday, August 2, 1942
9:17 a.m.
Outside the Randall Apartments, Washington, DC

Teresa Bryant packed what she needed for the weekend outing then dressed in slacks and a summer-weight cotton sweater. As she studied her suitcase, she spent a few minutes focusing on what she might expect from her trip. She picked up a legal pad and jotted down a few notes before exiting the Randall Apartments, a three-story, brick, furnished complex she'd moved into only ten days ago and strolled out on the sidewalk. Though she had no problem adapting on the run, Bryant was not by a nature a fly-by-the-seat-of-her-pants person. Her Caddo Indian heritage had instilled a desire to see what was on the horizon and to spend hours meditating on how to deal with it. Thus, there was rarely one specific plan, but rather many different ones that could be used as a situation developed and changed. So while the man who had issued the invitation would determine the destination, she would be ready to use several different paths to avoid his goals being realized.

There was a small park across the street and down the block—a spot where the local kids played and the elderly fed the pigeons. It might also be the perfect place to develop a plan to ward off North's assault while somehow maintaining his interest in her.

The first thing to determine was the best route to avoid the physical assault she was sure North was planning. He didn't invite her on this overnight trip just for conversation or to read the map, he had other things in mind. Thus, she had to stay in a position to control every moment.

The second thing on her agenda was to find out why the senator was making the trip. If the affair was cloaked in secrecy, he was not going to volunteer the nature of his meeting, so that meant she was going to use her own special skills to pry that information from him. That thought turned her stomach.

As she considered that bleak scenario, she stepped off the sidewalk between a 1936 Ford truck and 1939 Buick that were parked along the curb. A casual glance in both directions proved the street safe for crossing. She was three steps beyond the cars when she heard the screeching of rubber. A moment later she sensed more than saw a large, dark sedan lurch from the curb and speed toward her. The Cadillac's massive grill and fenders loomed not more than forty feet away, and the vehicle was closing fast. The look in the driver's eyes told her she was a target.

At that point, everything slowed down. To Bryant's eyes and mind, the oncoming car, as well as the people walking on the sidewalk, seemed to all but standstill. And it was during this time between the ticking seconds that Bryant's instincts kicked in.

As a child, she'd observed rabbits. When they saw a coyote rushing toward them those that froze died, as did those who attempted to employ a straight-line escape. But from time to time, a rabbit feinted one way and then reversed course. In many cases, the predator could not correct in time and rushed by the potential victim. Now was the time to be like the smart rabbits.

Bryant leaned forward and took a long step. The driver adjusted his course to compensate. As soon as the car shifted direction, Bryant spun and made a dive for the hood of the Ford truck parked along the curb. The Caddy readjusted, but a second too late. Rather than hitting its target, it clipped the Ford's driver's side front fender pushing the vehicle forward. Bryant was sprawled on the truck's hood when it struck the parked Buick. The collision gave her the chance to roll over the hood to the far fender and then drop to the sidewalk. Just as she landed, three shots breezed over her head and hit her apartment's brick wall. At that point, her assailant corrected his course and sped off.

"You okay?" a man walking a poodle asked.

Bryant rose to her feet and nodded. "I'm fine."

"What's going on with that guy?" the stranger asked.

"I have no idea," she lied.

In truth, she knew exactly what was going on. Bauer had hired someone to finish the job Fister could no longer do. She was just as sure this wouldn't be the last time the tall man tried to rub her out. Suddenly fighting off Jeb North seemed like the least of her worries. More than anything else, she had to stop Fredrick Bauer.

THE 13TH FLOOR

CHAPTER 24

Sunday, August 2, 1942
9:50 a.m.
Randall Apartments, Washington, DC

After dodging a few bullets and a speeding car, Teresa Bryant returned to her apartment, gathered her wits and changed out of the clothes she had been wearing. Dressed in a black, long-sleeved, high-necked blouse, matching slacks and flats, she left by cab to make her appointment with the senator. For the moment, she wanted to appear all business. So, unlike the night before, she wore minimal make-up and no perfume. She carried an overnight bag that contained her clothing and a make-up bag that included a thirty-two pistol, several pairs of handcuffs and another special weapon just in case North pushed too hard.

The trip to Titusville was largely uneventful. The senator filled the hours with stories about his life, and whenever he tried to shift the conversation in a more romantic direction, she asked another question on topics as varied as his childhood, his views on how long the war would last and who would win the American League. On two occasions, he also veered into his disdain for women in the workforce. Bryant didn't challenge him. Instead, she simply played along as if she agreed with everything he said.

They ate at a small Titusville diner called Nick's, before checking in at the two-story Stanford Arms Hotel. As North paid for their adjoining rooms, explaining that Bryant was his personal secretary, she studied a number of photographs hanging on the lobby's walls. Each was a different view of the oil industry that had once been the lifeblood of the area. Though the boom had ended decades before, apparently the town was still extremely proud of its petroleum heritage.

"Teresa," North called out, "we can go to our rooms now." He then smiled that smile of a man sure his plan was foolproof.

Bryant said nothing as North led the way up to rooms seven and nine. "This will be yours; mine is next door. I thought it was more proper that way. You go on in, and I'll see you in a few minutes."

Closing the door, Bryant studied the accommodations. The room was about fifteen by ten. There was a bed, dresser and one chair pushed under a desk. The only nightstand was on the right. The connecting bath was tiny but did have a full-sized tub. The walls were covered with paper that showed oil gushing from a derrick, thus keeping with the theme she noted in the lobby. The lamp beside the bed was also modeled after a derrick. The room's one window looked out over the community's central business district. One quick glance assured her none of the local establishments stayed open late. In fact, there was no one on the street at all. She was watching a cat trying to catch a cricket that had been attracted by a streetlamp when a knock on the connecting door signaled it was time for the battle.

Stepping to the entry, she opened it and found North waiting on the other side. With no warning, he moved close, kissed her and grinned.

Bryant leaned back, turned and posed a well-rehearsed question. "Is it really proper for us to be enjoying this moment when so many are fighting and dying in the name of freedom."

"That's why we need to enjoy it," he argued. "They're fighting for rights as well as our happiness. And that fight shows just how fragile life really is. You can never tell; this might be our only night together. So why waste it?"

She was contemplating how to answer when he issued a temporarily reprieve. "I wish I could stay for a while, but I have meeting."

"At this time of night?" Bryant asked. "And why couldn't you have just called the person from Washington?"

"Because," he explained, "there are some things that shouldn't be discussed on the phone."

That gave her all the information she needed to know. This was not about some piece of legislation; this was something that North couldn't afford to air in public. That's why he had made this seemingly unnecessary trip.

"Anyway," he continued, "it shouldn't take too long. When I finish, I'll knock on your door, and we can get to know each other even better."

She knew what he meant, but as she had come prepared, she wasn't worried either. With a fake smile framing her face, she watched North walk down the hall to the stairs and go up. She quietly followed a few seconds later.

At the top of the stairwell, she peaked around the corner and noted the senator lightly knocking on a door. After it opened, she stole down the hall to room twenty-seven. She leaned close enough to hear voices, but she couldn't make out what they were saying. Turning, she rushed down the stairs, through the lobby and to the back of the building. Just as she had hoped, there was a fire escape outside the room's window. After making sure no one was watching, she silently pulled down the ladder, climbed to a point just outside the window and crouched beside it. Now she could clearly hear the conversation and it was easy to tell that North was not a happy man.

"We've had too many deaths," the senator snapped. "Way too many. There were more than sixty in Chicago last week."

"You told me not to worry about anything other than making sure the authorities couldn't trace it to arson. You said nothing about how many died. In fact, you told me you needed a few deaths to stir the pot. Those were your words, not mine."

Bryant carefully leaned forward and peeked in. The other man was slightly built, appearing to be about forty, with small hands and narrow shoulders. Dressed in slacks and a white shirt, he looked as if he could have been a salesman. As she noted North coming toward the window, she pulled back and pushed flat against the wall.

"Okay, fine you were following my directives," the senator agreed, but it's gone a bit overboard. We just need to be careful about how many lives we take from now on in."

"How many more of these do we need before you can get what you want?" the man demanded.

Bryant looked down and noted North's fingers grip the bottom on the partially open window. "It's hot in here," the senator grumbled as he pulled the glass upward.

If he leaned out, Bryant would sure she would be spotted. As she inventoried her limited escape routes, she pressed even more deeply into the wall. Just to her right, she spotted a downspout. Reaching over the edge of the fire escape, she wrapped her fingers onto the downspout and swung. She was shocked but grateful when it held her weight. Now dangling twenty feet above the brick alley, she reached up with her free hand and grabbed the metal guttering above her head. Taking a deep breath, she pulled herself up until she was eye level with the flat roof. As she hung there, she glanced down and noted North step through the window onto the fire escape platform. She was lucky! For the moment, he was looking forward. Using all her strength, she silently reached forward with her right hand and grabbed a metal exhaust pipe. Using it for leverage, she pulled the top half of her body over the gutter and rolled forward until she was safely on the roof. She lay on her back for a moment, caught her breath, then flipped over and crawled back to where she was just above the window. Lying flat on her stomach, she waited for North to speak.

"You need a fan," the senator announced as he crawled back into the room.

"I'll make a note of that," the other man replied.

"This rising body count has me nervous," North continued. "Maybe we need to call tonight off. Give things for a rest for a few weeks."

"Too late," the stranger explained. "The timer's already counting down. The bomb goes off at 2:00 a.m. That's a bit more than three hours."

"It's at the Slippery Rock Refinery?" North asked.

"Yep."

"How many people are working there tonight?"

"Because it's Sunday, only a cleaning crew. So just five women will go up with the blast."

"Okay," the senator's tone indicated a sense of relief, "the fact there will be no men present means we can still shift the blame to women. That will help me push the bill to remove females from all war-related factory positions. If I don't nip this right now, within two years, we will have ten to twenty million women in positions that should be reserved for men."

"You've made it clear you don't want that," the bomb maker observed.

"But we still need to slow down a bit," North explained. "Let's hold off on the next explosion until I determine how much leverage I have. If I can get enough senators on my side, then we might not have to plant any more bombs."

"Hey, I'm not a man of conscience, but this is a bizarre way to get what you want."

"It's not what I want," the Senator explained. "I hate the fact people are dying. But in this case, they are dying for a good cause so I can live with it. It's simply not good for society to have women in positions where they work with men. Worse yet, imagine a world where men were bossed by women. It would be chaos. These people are dying so we can keep the world as it was intended to be. We have to maintain that line between the sexes and their roles intact or chaos will reign."

"Okay," came the response, "If you feel that way, I can live with it. But if we don't have any more bombings, then

I'll be losing some promised paychecks. So if we put things on hold, do I still get paid?"

"Yeah," North promised. "And here's what I owe you tonight. Now, are you sure no one connects you with these jobs?"

"I'm a salesman," he explained. "I stop in hundreds of places each year. I sell them cleaning supplies and deliver them from my truck. Most of those spots don't have explosions. And, on top of that, no one can actually pin this on arson or sabotage. That's how good I am."

"Okay, I have a young woman waiting on me. Remember no more fireworks until you hear from me."

"Got it."

After hearing the room's door open and close, Bryant crawled to the edge of the roof, grabbed the gutter with both hands and swung over until she was hanging two feet above the fire escape landing. She then dropped quietly to the platform and rushed down the ladder to the alley. Once there, she entered the hotel through the rear door and checked the hall. North was walking toward their rooms, but rather than stop, he went on to the lobby. Seizing the moment, Bryant raced down the hall, opened her door, closed and locked it as well as entry connecting the two rooms. After taking a deep breath, she hurried into the bathroom and checked the mirror. She had dirt on her face, hands and clothing and her hair was a mess. Stripping off her blouse and slacks, she went to work attempting to look as if she hadn't left her room. Three minutes later, just as she removed the last bit of grime off her hands, there was a knock on the connecting door. Running a brush through her hair, she grabbed a silk robe, tossed it on and tied it. After a final glance into the mirror, she stepped forward and unlocked the door.

North stood there in slacks and a shirt holding a bottle of scotch and two glasses. As he noted Bryant's silk robe, he smiled. "I see our minds are moving in the same direction. I hope I haven't kept you waiting too long?"

"No," she assured him as she took his glasses, "I was happy to have the time to slip into something a bit more comfortable. Why don't you go sit down on the bed? I'll open the bottle and pour our drinks."

As the smiling senator turned, Bryant set the glasses and bottle onto her sink ledge, slipped her hand into her make-up bag and retrieved a small container filled with white power. She opened it, tapped about a teaspoon into one of the glasses, added the liquor and watched the power dissolve. She then filled the other glass, waltzed back to North's side, pushed a drink toward her guest and grinned.

After allowing his eyes to enjoy her charms, he took the glass and offered a toast, "To good days and better nights."

A second later, the glass was empty. After setting it on the nightstand, he reached for the woman. Pulling her onto his lap, he kissed her deeply. Bryant allowed that kiss and several others before standing.

"What are you doing?" he demanded. "The fun is just beginning."

"Just watching you," she explained.

"I want you," he demanded. "Come to me."

"Let me spray on some perfume first," she suggested.

She felt his eyes follow her across the room. As she pulled the bottle from her bag, North called out. "Just being with you makes me dizzy. I've never had a woman do this to me before."

She turned and smiled, "I'll bet you haven't."

As his eyes rolled back, his mouth formed a silly grin and then a few seconds later, he fell back onto the bed. Bryant strolled to his side and lightly slapped him on the cheek. There was no response. If her calculations were right, he would be out for a bit over an hour. That would give her the time she needed to get ready for action.

CHAPTER 25

Monday, August 3, 1942
12:03 a.m.
Stanford Arms Hotel, Titusville, Pennsylvania

After dressing in slacks, a dark blouse and flats, Teresa Bryant walked into the senator's room, found the man's keys and billfold, and casually strolled down to the hotel's parking lot. Finding North's stretch-Lincoln sedan, she started the car and drove it back to the alley. After making a couple of adjustments to the dash, she stole into the hotel through the back door and cautiously walked through the building checking for activity. There was none. Even the desk clerk was napping in a chair behind the main counter.

Back in her own room, Bryant took North's left wrist, looked at this watch, pulled out the stem and reset the time. Grabbing the tall man under his arms, she pulled him off the bed, dragged him to the door, opened it, and, after making sure no one was in the hall, pulled the senator to the hotel's back door and out to the car. Setting him in the passenger side front seat, she hurried back to her room and retrieved her make-up bag. Returning to the car, she pulled a pair of handcuffs out of the bag and clamped North's left wrist to the door. Sliding behind the wheel, she checked her watch; she had a couple of hours to accomplish her task. She would be cutting it close, but it was worth the effort. If this went well, she would save a few lives and expose a sick plot devised by a very insecure, narrow-minded man. Bryant hit the starter and slipped the car into first, but before she could pull away, she heard a voice. Startled she looked to both sides and checked her review mirror. There was no one around. Then she heard it again.

"Car 17, check out a hitchhiker on Route 8."

A relieved Bryant looked beneath the dash to the police radio. She wondered how she could have missed noticing it on the drive up. When she'd pulled North into the car, his body must have hit the toggle switch. Flipping it back to the off position, she drove by a large janitorial supply truck and headed toward the Slippery Rock Refinery.

There was no traffic on the road, and the trip was uneventful. Most importantly, her passenger continued to sleep like a baby.

It was 12:24 when she pulled up to the facility's main gate. A short, thin, older man dressed in a uniform stepped out of a guardhouse and walked toward the car. As he approached Bryant reached for her gun and another pair of handcuffs, opened the door and slid out of the Lincoln.

"What's you need, lady?"

"I need to use your phone. The man in the car is Senator Jeb North, I'm his aide, and I think he just had a heart attack."

The old man looked into the car. "Say, he don't look very good. Come on, I've got one in the guardhouse." Bryant followed the man inside. "There it is on my desk."

"Thanks," she said as she revealed the weapon. "Now, I don't want to hurt you, so you're going to need to sit down in that chair with your arms behind your back."

After noting the gun, the guard didn't protest. Bryant produced the handcuffs and locked the man in place. She glanced around the office until she saw a jacket. After ripping off an arm, she gagged the man and then yanked the phone cord out of the wall.

"I'm sorry," she explained, "in time, you'll understand I'm actually saving your life."

After opening the gate, she slid back into the car and pulled it into the plant. After parking the vehicle beside a gasoline storage tank, she turned off the Lincoln's V-12 engine and began to gently slap North's cheeks. It took a few minutes, but he finally came around.

"Hey," he moaned, "what goes on here?"

"You're at the Slippery Rock Refinery," Bryant calmly explained.

The news immediately pushed all the fog out of the man's brain. Moving his head as if it were on a swivel, he squirmed like a schoolboy at his first dance.

"What time is it?" he demanded as he tried to yank his right arm free from the cuffs.

"Look at the clock on the dash," she suggested.

"My Lord, we only have five minutes to get out of here!" His tone was frantic.

"What do you mean by that?" she demanded.

"This whole plant goes up at two. There's a bomb in there!" he announced as he leaned his head toward the facility's production facility.

As Bryant coolly studied the large, brick complex, North looked at the time on his watch. "Come on, let's move."

"Where's the bomb?" Bryant demanded.

"I don't know," a sweating North quickly replied. "I don't know where or even how it's set up. I just know what time it goes off."

Bryant nodded. She should have realized he wouldn't know. Still having him here sweating it out brought her an immense sense of pleasure.

"Who are you?" he asked.

"Your worse nightmare," she announced as she brought her gun's butt to the side of his head.

Satisfied North was again asleep, Bryant reset the dashboard's clock to the right time and did the same to North's watch. It was just past one. That meant she had less than an hour to find the bomb. She was just about to open the door and begin searching the plant when she saw headlights.

CHAPTER 26

Monday, August 3, 1942
1:07 a.m.
Slippery Rock Refinery outside Titusville, Pennsylvania

A tall man, dressed in dark slacks and a white shirt stepped out of a 1942 Olds sedan. Behind him, a yellow 1937 Packard slowed to a stop. A few seconds later, Helen Meeker joined the nervous stranger.

"I wonder where Bill is?" the man asked. "First, you get me out of bed in the middle of the night, and now Bill's nowhere in sight. What's going on?"

"Our problem is not Bill," Meeker suggested, "I'm pretty certain that someone is going to try to blow up your plant in the next few days. You're going to have to strengthen security?"

The man turned to face his guest, "And where do I get the men. I can barely find enough able bodies to staff this facility. Half my line workers are women for heaven's sake, and most of the others have come out retirement."

A flash of light caused Meeker's eyes to move from the plant's owner to a car parked to her right. A woman dressed in dark clothing slowly emerged from the shadows.

"Helen Meeker, fancy meeting you here."

"Teresa?"

"Yeah, and you don't have to worry about extra security, I've found out there's a bomb already planted here, and it's scheduled to go off at two."

"What?" the stunned man demanded more than asked.

As she checked her watch, Meeker made the introductions. "Teresa Bryant this is Walter Silverstein. He owns this plant. Silverstein, Teresa works with the FBI."

"Doesn't anyone use men anymore?" he moaned.

"Nice meeting you too," Bryant spat out her sarcastic reply before turning to the other woman. "Helen, your theory was right. The man who asked me on the trip is behind this. And it's for all the reasons you thought. He's over in the car sleeping like a baby because he couldn't tell me where the bomb is located."

"Where's the best place to put a bomb in your plant?" a cool Meeker asked as she assimilated the new information.

"Obviously by a tank or feeder pipe," Silverstein explained.

"If we can find it," Bryant chimed in, "I'm pretty sure I can defuse it. By the way, do you know if a janitorial supply truck visited the refinery recently?"

Silverstein balled up his hands and screamed, "Like that's important at this moment. Lady, there's a bomb and enough gasoline around you right now to blow us into kingdom come."

"Just answer the question?" Bryant demanded.

Silverstein looked to Meeker but got the same respond. "Answer her. Were there any deliveries recently?"

"As a matter of fact," the owner explained, "I had to come out and let a guy in today. He normally comes the first Monday of the month but explained he had to be in New York tomorrow. So I agreed to meet him. But I don't see …"

"I'll explain in a second," Bryant assured him. "Now, do you know what he delivered?"

"As we didn't work today, I was the one who accepted the order and even helped him unload the stuff. But who cares? We have a bomb to find!"

"Why don't you fill me," Meeker suggested to Bryant as she ignored Silverstein's pleas.

"Here's the score, Helen. The guy who sets up the explosions is a janitorial product salesman. It's the perfect cover for entry into the plants. The device that triggers the explosion must be hidden in the products he delivers."

"But we've been using him for over a year," the owner argued.

"And," Meeker noted, "That has bought him the time to gain your trust. Now, you said you helped unload the order."

"Yeah, the stuff is inside the main building in our supply room. No one has even had a chance to use it yet."

"Then you need to take us there now," Bryant suggested.

With the almost frantic man hurriedly leading the way, the trio entered the refinery via a side entry, made a right through a break room and down a hall. Silverstein then reached for his keys and unlocked a door. After flipping a light switch, he walked into the large supply room.

"That's what we unloaded," he announced while pointing to a stack of cans, bottles, and boxes to his right.

"Were you with him the whole time?" Bryant asked.

"No," he explained, "I helped him bring it in, then he had some paperwork he needed to do, so I went back to my office. I saw his truck leave exactly five minutes later. I know because I checked the time on my watch when I left the room, and I checked it again when I heard the truck start up. I'm a fanatic about knowing the time. Have been since I got my first watch as a kid."

Meeker frowned. "And no one else was here?"

"Just the security guard. The cleaning crew doesn't come in until about six."

"Now," Meeker ordered, "look at that stuff and tell me if that contains everything the two of you brought in."

"I can be sure it is," Silverstein explained, "our head janitor has a checklist that he fills out, and it's placed on the clipboard hanging on the back of the door. Because it was Sunday, I did that inventory. I'll grab the board and check over the items."

"You said two?" Meeker asked as her eyes meet Bryant's.

"Yeah, and that means we have less than forty minutes to find the bomb."

"Teresa, do you think he could have gone back to the truck and retrieved it after Silverstein left?"

"No, it took us two minutes to walk back to the room. And we were moving at a good clip. That means it would have taken the bomber that long, plus, he would have had to place it near something combustible, set the timer and get back to the truck. So it has to have been a part of the delivery."

"There's a box of detergent missing," Silverstein announced causing both women to swing around. "We always order five boxes, and only four of them are here."

Meeker pointed to four two-foot-high orange cardboard boxes. "Like that?" She then turned to Byrant and asked, "What do you think?"

"It's doesn't take a big bomb to set off a huge explosion in a refinery. He could easily hide what he needs in a soap box."

"So my whole plant is about to blow up?" he whispered.

To be certain she now had the frightened man's full attention, Meeker grabbed Silverstein by the shoulders. She looked directly into his eyes as she spoke. "How many employees are here right now?"

"Four elderly cleaning ladies and our guard."

"Round them up and get them as are far from here as you can. I suggest you take them to your home so they don't tell anyone what's going on. I'll call you if we find the bomb and get it defused. And if we don't, you and everyone with twenty miles will know."

Bryant reached into her pocket and retrieved a key. "You'll need this to free your guard. He's in his little house. And before you leave, flip on every light in the place."

After the plant's owner took the key and darted off, Meeker turned to the other woman. "Where do we start?"

"I think we split up and looked at every volatile spot in the main building. If he's trying to make it look like this was caused by a plant worker, that's where they would set it up."

"But the massive storage tanks are easier targets," Meeker pointed out.

"Yeah," Bryant agreed, "but this is about targeting female workers, and I'll bet none of them drive trucks. That's still considered a man's job. We only have about twenty minutes to locate that orange box. We need to move."

Meeker rushed into the main building to find herself surrounded by hundreds of miles of pipe and more tanks than she could count. Trying to stay focused, she hurried across the concrete floor, looking under worktables, behind vats, and around pipes. From one huge four-story room to the next she raced as five minutes became ten. When she hit the back wall, she reversed course and retraced her steps. But there was no orange box. Pausing at the place she had begun, she rubbed her mouth and looked back at the plant. That was when she noticed a women's restroom right behind a twenty-four-inch supply line. Hurrying over, she threw open the door, turned on the light and spotted an empty orange soapbox tossed on its side in the corner. Crouching down, she studied the room. Under the sink, chained to a metal wall brace, was a small device consisting of a clock, two sticks of dynamite and a bottle of clear liquid. She checked her watch. It was now 1:52.

Stepping out of the small room, Meeker yelled out, "I've found it!"

"I'm on my way," a voice called back. A minute later, Bryant raced up.

"It's under the sink."

The brunette fell to her knees and studied the device. Leaning closer she sighed. "This is just great."

"What?" Meeker asked as she leaned closer and noted the clock's second hand moving at what seemed to be light speed.

"Normally a time bomb is set up with two or three wires. You trace them back to see which one is the trigger and cut it. If you cut the wrong one, the device explodes. This guy set this one up with a dozen wires. Only one of them matters, the rest are literally false leads, but it will take a long time to trace each one and figure out the one to cut. And once again, if I guess wrong, we will be playing harps. Or at least, you will be, I'm not so sure what instrument they'll give me." She paused as if to gauge her situation before looking toward Meeker. "There are tool benches all around the main plant, find me some wire snips."

Meeker rushed out, grabbed the clippers and returned to Bryant. They now had less than five minutes to deactivate the bomb.

"Thanks," Bryant said as she took the tool. "Now, you have time to get out of here. I'd suggest driving as fast as you can because when this goes off, they'll find bricks and pieces of steel three miles away."

"I'm staying," Meeker resolutely announced. "I got you into this, and I'll ride it out with you."

"Fly might be a better word," Bryant wryly cracked. "Okay, I've found three that are false leads. Now there're only nine to go."

Bryant was perched on her knees, snips in her right hand, as she traced the wires with her left. It took a minute to identify another dummy. It was now 1:59.

"I'm just going to have to guess," she whispered, "and the odds are still way too long. If you know any prayers, say them quick."

There were less than thirty seconds before the sweep second hand pushed to twelve and the clock struck two. As a hesitant Bryant moved the snips from one wire to another, Meeker fell to her knees, reached behind the bomb and found one of the clock's time adjusting keys.

"How about we try this?" Meeker suggested as she moved the big hand back thirty-five minutes. Three ticks later, the second hand swept past twelve, and nothing happened.

"Why didn't you do that earlier?" Bryant asked as she wiped the sweat from her forehead.

"Why didn't you?" Meeker countered.

"Helen, you do realize that if Hollywood finds out all you have to do is wind the clock backward, it's going to ruin a lot of down-to-the-wire adventure movies? After all, the ticking clock bomb is a tried and proven plot device. This might change the entire adventure movie industry." She shook her head, "I still can't believe worked."

"We bought some time," Meeker noted, "but we still need to move it out of here."

"Let's get a hacksaw and cut the chain," Bryant suggested. "Then we can take it out in the country, drop it in a field and let it go off on its own."

Meeker pushed herself off her knees. "I'll get a saw."

Five minutes later, Meeker had cut halfway through a link in the chain.

"Let me take over," Bryant suggested.

"Okay, that'll be fine. I saw a phone back in the break room. I'll call Silverstein and tell him we saved his plant. When you get that thing free, take it out and put it in the car. Then we can drive out and get rid of it."

Meeker had just hung up the line when Bryant stuck her head in the break room door. "You ready?"

"Do you have the bomb in the car?"

"Resting on the backseat floor," she assured Meeker. "And we have about twenty minutes to spare."

The now relaxed pair made their way to the side entrance. As Bryant opened the door and stepped out into the open, a shot rang out, hitting the door frame just above her head. Meeker reached up, hit the light switch, bathing the area in darkness, and fell to the ground.

"Who shot at us?"

"It came from the Lincoln," Bryant noted. "It has to be North. I checked on him when I dropped off the bomb, and he appeared to be out like a light. He must have just come to. My guess is there was gun hidden under the seat or dash. I should have thought to check for that."

When Meeker pushed the door slightly ajar to gauge the situation, two more shots rang out. "Yes, you should have checked, and North is very much awake now. His aim seems to be getting better too."

"He's likely trying to free his right arm from where I cuffed him to the door."

"Well," Meeker noted, "we can't play this game forever. When the clock finally strikes two, we're going to learn how to fly. How much time do we have now?"

"About fifteen minutes."

"We can't make it to the car, it's too far. We would be sitting ducks for him if we tried. We also can't shoot at him because of the storage tank. If a bullet hit that monster, we'd create a new way to set off our bomb."

"Let's give him a few minutes," Bryant suggested. "My guess is he'll find a way to pulled the handcuffs of the door."

"Then what?"

"We let him drive out."

"And Teresa, what if it doesn't happen in time?"

"Then we make a run for it and hope he runs out of lead."

Meeker rolled over on her back as a minute became two and then five. "How much time now?"

"Seven minutes," Bryant answered.

"Any regrets?"

"Yeah, one."

"What's that?"

"I should have parked the Lincoln someplace else."

"My only regret," Meeker added, "is that no one will ever find out how brilliant I was when I moved the minute hand back thirty-five minutes."

"Yeah," Bryant cracked, "you should have run it back an hour."

"I hear something!" Meeker exclaimed as she rolled to her feet and opened the door a crack. "There's a truck rolling through the gate. For a night off, this place sure gets a lot of business."

Bryant peaked out. "It's the bomb maker. I'm guessing North used his radio to contact him."

The truck rolled to a stop between the women and the Lincoln. A few seconds later, the driver slid across the cab and exited on the passenger side.

"He'll be able to get North free," Meeker noted.

"Bryant pulled her gun from her purse and smiled. "But they're not using that truck for an escape."

"You can't shoot," Meeker argued. "What if you miss and hit the tank."

"With the time running down, it's worth risk."

"Think about this," Meeker cut in. "We want them to leave so that we can ditch that bomb."

Steadying her hand, Bryant ignored the other woman's observations, aimed and pulled her trigger. A split second later, the truck's rear tire began losing air. She repeated the action and flattened the front tire. With a confused Meeker looking on, Bryant watched and waited.

Meeker frowned. "Now I want to live just so I can point out how stupid that was."

"How much time we have?" Bryant asked.

"Four minutes. You ready to make a run for the car?"

"Not yet."

From behind the truck, the Lincoln's V-12 came to life, and the huge sedan lurched forward, slowly circling around the now-wounded vehicle. As it moved away from their position, Bryant stood and opened the door, her dark eyes following the vehicle as it sped up.

Stepping out, Meeker raised her gun and aimed. "I can safely get a shot now."

"Don't," Bryant shouted, "let them go."

Lowering her Colt, Meeker raced toward the Packard. "We have a bomb to dispose of," she yelled, "and we have less than three minutes to get it out of the plant."

Bryant turned her gaze from the now disappearing Lincoln to her watch. "Actually, it's only two."

"Come on," a frantic Meeker yelled.

"No reason to hurry," Bryant argued.

"But the bomb?"

"I put on the Lincoln's rear floorboard. Senator North is disposing of it for us. I'm guessing it will be his final bit of service for his country."

Still not fully believing Bryant, Meeker glanced into the Packard's rear floorboard. There was nothing there. A few seconds later, a loud roar filled the air, and a large fireball appeared on the horizon.

CHAPTER 27

Wednesday, August 5, 1942
9:15 a.m.
Office of the Director, FBI Building, Washington, DC

Sam Lake, a sixty-year-old, ten-year veteran of the FBI, purposely walked up to Teresa Bryant's desk. Lake's clear green eyes caught the woman's as he used his head to signal for her to follow him into the director's office. Once the short but solid man shut the door, he pointed to a chair. Bryant said nothing as she sat down.

"You were with North when he died?" Lake began.

The woman coyly smiled, "Actually, if I had been with him when he died, I would have died too. If you read my report, you know I was at the hotel."

Lake frowned. "The White House is reporting the senator died saving the Slippery Rock Refinery from sabotage. Do you know anything about that?"

"I've read the newspapers," she quipped, "and we all know that only the truth makes its way to print."

She crossed her leg, folded her hands over her lap and waited for the next question. As she did her interrogator moved to the window and studied the Capitol.

"Miss Bryant," he didn't turn to face her as he posed his question, "how did you get home from Titusville?"

"I caught a ride," she explained. "As my being with the senator might seem unseemly, I thought it best to get out of town as quickly as possible."

Lake turned and with a stern look asked, "Was it unseemly?"

"A lady never tells," she shot back, "and besides a gentleman has no business asking. By the way, are you a gentleman, Mr. Lake?"

Lake pointed to a folder on Hoover's desk. "Our reports clearly spell out that North was no hero. There's something else at work here, and you know what it is."

"Do I?"

"Miss Bryant!"

"Listen, if you must know, I was not having an affair with North, though that's what he wanted. Secondly, I was obviously not with him when he died. Lastly, my getting out of Titusville when I did kept the FBI out of the newspapers. Now, what else does J. Edgar want to know that he was afraid to ask me himself?"

"Talk like that will get your fired," Lake warned.

"I could always get a job in a refinery," she quipped. "I understand the pay is better than what I make here." She raised her eyebrow. "Is there anything else?"

"Why was North in Titusville? Why did he visit the plant?"

"He only told me he had a meeting, I wasn't invited to it. But based on the outcome, I'm guessing he got wind of the sabotage and was trying to stop it."

Lake pounded his fist on the desk. "Then why didn't he call us?"

"Because," Bryant pointed out, "the Bureau saw this as nothing more than a series of accidents. No one looked upon this as sabotage. Therefore, you would have ignored him, and another plant would have gone up in smoke. Would you like me to paint that picture to the press?"

Lake crossed his arms over his chest and frowned. "If you didn't like him, why did you go with him?"

"I went because I had evidence the Pennsylvania plant would be the next to go up," she lied. "As the only one in the FBI who thought that way, I figured I could dig up a little information. If you will check with the plant manager, I actually figured out who the bomber was. I didn't get to stop him because North gave his life saving the facility."

"And," Lake spat, "Silverstein said you were working with Helen Meeker."

"She arrived after I did," Bryant corrected him. "I had no idea she was in the area."

"But she gave you a ride home."

"Yes."

"What did she tell you?" he demanded.

"We discussed fashion and music," Bryant explained. "I'm into reds and blues, she prefers greens and grays."

"What else?"

"We're women, what else would you expect us to discuss?" Bryant added with more than a hint of sarcasm. "Now what's the real story here? Why are you grilling me?"

"The director doesn't like you getting close to anyone at the White House."

"So, Hoover thinks it's all right for me to use my looks and brains to serve his seedy needs, but I can't get the credit for solving cases, and I can't develop friendships with interesting people he doesn't care for."

"He doesn't mind you pretending to be Meeker's friend," Lake added, "but only if you dig up the information we need to take her down."

"Why would you want to take her down?" she demanded.

"The director doesn't like or trust the woman."

"That's likely true," Bryant quipped. "But the real problem here is that Helen Meeker scares him. Every time he has tried to put her in her place, she's made him look stupid. She has more gumption and guile than anyone in this department. She can out think any of you." The woman grinned, "She's more a man than you or Hoover will ever be. So I'm not going to do anything to bring her down."

"If that's the case," Lake barked, "then you need to pack your things and get out of here."

"I had an offer this morning," Bryant announced as she stood, "and you helped me decide to take it. Mr. Lake, you best watch your back because there are skeletons in your closet. In fact, I have dirt on almost everyone here. Be sure Mr. Hoover knows that."

Smiling, Bryant winked and exited the office and the FBI.

CHAPTER 28

Wednesday, August 5, 1942
7:15 p.m.
Grant Hotel, Washington, DC

As she studied her small quarters, Helen Meeker made a mental note to spend tomorrow trying to find an apartment. But with the current housing shortage, that was going to be a real problem. Perhaps this time, her new found fame might work in her favor. Perhaps being the Queen of the Press might actually serve a good purpose for a change.

Though she wasn't hungry, it was time to eat. But eating alone had quickly become an exercise in futility. Because of her star status, everyone wanted to meet her, have a picture made or get an autograph. How she longed for the days when she was "dead."

Meeker was shocked when a simple twist of the knob and pull of the door revealed a young woman standing outside in the hall. The visitor, dressed in a British military uniform, looked uncomfortable and lost.

"Gail," Meeker announced. "I really didn't expect to see you again."

"Probably didn't want to," came the apologetic reply. "I didn't know that my Henry had once been yours. I need you to believe that."

"I'm sure you didn't," Meeker said with a forced smile. "After all, the man that I loved died, and your love is very much alive. Why don't you come in?"

Worel stiffly marched past her host and found a chair. Only after Meeker was seated did the visitor pick up the awkward conversation.

"I don't feel right taking Henry from you. He was yours first."

Meeker took no time correcting her visitor. "No, he wasn't. I had the chance to make him mine and passed on it. What Henry and I had is therefore in the past. From what I've been told, you're in love with him, and he is very much in love with you. That is the now and that's what matters."

"But …"

"No buts," Meeker announced. "Maybe if it weren't for this crazy war, I'd try to win him back, but Henry can't be seen with me. You see as far as the world is concerned, he's a ghost. He needs to stay a ghost. That way he can go back underground and help this war get over that much sooner."

Worel shook head. "That's very noble of you."

"No," she corrected the visitor, "You see, when it comes to affairs of the heart, I wrote them off to try to be more than anyone expected a woman could be. It was my choice. So it wasn't a noble choice, it was one based on my somewhat selfish desires and ambitions."

The room was silent as the pair searched for the words to clear air that would likely never again be clear. As the seconds dragged on, both looked everywhere but at each other.

"We're leaving tonight," Worel finally explained. "I couldn't go without facing you."

"Thanks," Meeker answered, "but you owe me nothing. I respect you as a woman and a soldier. I also wish you the best of luck. In this crazy world we live in, you will need it."

Worel stood, walked back to the room's entry and then turned back to her host. Their eyes met, and the Brit announced, "You are a remarkable woman, Helen." A few seconds later, she opened the door and walked out.

It felt like a funeral, even though it was really a confirmation of life and love. Only the ringing of the phone kept away the tears and mourning.

"Helen Meeker."

"It's Vance."

She was glad for the call. She needed a distraction in the worst possible way.

"What do you need, Dizzy? You still in Chicago?"

"Yeah, but I'm about to be on my way back. Thanks to a new source, I've dug up some good stuff on the people behind the black market in the Midwest."

"Good, sounds like a matter for the FBI. Why don't you give the material to Alison and let her use our channels to pass it on?"

"I'll do that," Vance replied, "but there's something else my source gave me that might direct us to the man who was pulling Fister's strings."

"Okay," Meeker cut in, "now that's news I want to hear. What do you have?"

"Helen, it seems that the tall, dark stranger had a connection to Carfono and now O'Toole. They call him Darkness."

Meeker smiled. "How much new information do you have?"

"More than we did. He has connections with organized crime, the Nazis, and even the FBI."

"Playing all the sides," she quipped. "Does your source know whose side he's on now?"

"His own."

"Listen, Dizzy, I'm supposed to meet the President in Warm Springs on Friday. Can you be there too?"

"I'll bring the information. See you there."

"Thank you, Lord," Meeker whispered as she set the receiver back into the cradle.

Her words were sincere. Having something to work on might be the only way to forget all she had lost.

CHAPTER 29

Friday, August 7, 1942
2:15 p.m.
Little White House, Warm Springs, Georgia

Helen Meeker, dressed in slacks and a light blue blouse, waited in the small home's study for the President. As she fanned herself with a newspaper, she thought over the information Dizzy Vance shared that morning.

Darkness was no doubt the man behind Fister, but he wasn't an ardent Nazi, he was more like a freelance operator who saw war as a chance to gain power and make money. It was ironic she'd just dealt with two senators who used the same business model. And, as she thought about it, Darkness was likely no more deadly than they were.

Grabbing a pen from the desk, she began to sketch the image of the eyes she had seen staring at her outside of Grace Lupino's apartment. They were dark, cold and evil. It was as if they had been dreamed up for an Edgar Allan Poe short story. As she shaped them with the pencil, she realized for the first time the two deep pools reflected death more than life. "You taking up art?"

Meeker looked up as a valet, Arthur Pettyman, rolled the President into the room. Once the wheelchair was positioned directly in front of her, Pettyman nodded and left.

"No," Meeker replied, "I was wasting some time."

"If you were thinking," her host noted, "and you usually are, then you weren't wasting your time."

"Did you look at Dizzy Vance's report?" the woman asked.

"I did, and the FBI is involved in taking down the black market operators even as we speak."

"What about the other information he was able to get?"

"From the source inside the O'Toole gang?"

"Yes."

"Darkness."

"What are your thoughts?" Meeker asked.

"In truth," the President began, "his type might just be a bigger danger than those who are waging war against us. I've come to believe that personal ambition, when not controlled by morality, defines evil in ways that few can begin to imagine."

"Are you talking about Jeb North and Andrew Melon?"

"They are two of many," the President pointed out. "But Darkness is more dangerous because he's underground and is playing all sides against the middle. He has no allegiance to anyone. Worst of all, I'm sure he has contacts right here in Washington doing his bidding. They are likely walking the halls of Congress, in the military and even in the White House. If he controlled Fister, then he was behind the plot to kill Winston and myself."

"Does that mean I can go after him?" Meeker asked hopefully.

"Yes," he agreed, "as the public cannot know about this kind of evil, and as I don't know who in the FBI might be connected to Darkness, this will be your job. You have Dizzy's information, so you have a starting point."

"But," Helen argued, "O'Toole didn't know who Darkness was or where he is headquartered. So how do I start?"

"You will start in Chicago. For the duration of the war, you'll have a suite of rooms in the Grant Hotel. Your number will be 1217. The key and the all information you'll need are in a package you'll receive after this meeting.

"Why Chicago?"

"Because it's a midway point between both coasts with excellent travel connections. It's also away from Washington. That'll remove you from this fishbowl and make it far easier to work. After all, you are quite a celebrity here."

"I'm tired of being a media darling," she admitted, "but how can I work out of a hotel room? If I need a lab, what can I use?"

"You'll have a lab at your headquarters that will include everything you need."

"My suite is that large?"

"Hardly," the President explained. "But you'll have the entire 13th floor for you headquarters."

"I've been to the Grant," she argued, "there is no 13th floor."

"No, there is a 13th floor, the elevator and stairs just don't get you there. In your suite, you will find a hidden panel. Your packet will explain how to work it. Open that panel, march up the steps and you will be in your secret headquarters. In fact, we have lots of secret headquarters on the 13th floors of buildings. We even have an American team operating on the 13th floor of the Hotel Berlin. You see, even Hitler and the SS don't realize those floors exist. And they exist for a reason."

After gaining some mental traction, she looked back to her boss. "Do you expect me to do this on my own?"

"No," he assured her. "Vance will work with you when you need him. He has developed a source close to O'Toole who will help. And I have assigned another very capable person to your team."

"Who?" Meeker asked.

The President smiled, turned his chair and pushed it over to the door. After twisting a lock, he backed off, and the entry swung open.

"Miss Bryant, I think you've met Miss Meeker."

"What?" a shocked Meeker asked.

"Miss Bryant knows Darkness," the President explained, "and she knows where his headquarters are."

The woman quickly corrected the world's most powerful man. "Were … he has cleared out of his farm. But I think by searching through the home, barn, and lab, we might find clues as to where he is heading next."

"How do you know Teresa?" a still stunned Meeker demanded of the most powerful man on earth.

"She's been in my service for some time," the President explained. "In fact, she has served several presidents."

"What do you mean by that?" Meeker asked. "That makes no sense at all."

"All in good time, my dear," came the reply. "For the moment, you need to pack your things and get to the Windy City. The two of you have a mission that's likely more vital to the future peace of this world than it is to our current war. God bless you and God's speed."

The two women watched the President wheel out of the small office. Once he was gone, Meeker posed a question.

"Were you assigned to look out for me? Because I'll resent that until the day I die. In fact, if that's the case I'll never forgive the President!"

"No," Bryant quickly assured her, "you never needed a babysitter. I was working different cases, and we just happen to run into each other from time to time. Months ago, I was assigned to find Darkness because he had a direct interest in something I knew about. So here's the pitch. Darkness's real name is Bauer and by getting to know him, I discovered his mole at the FBI."

"Did you kill that mole?" Meeker demanded.

"Not directly," came her cryptic reply.

"What does that mean?"

"It just means he died looking like a hero," Bryant explained, "and I had nothing to do with putting lead through his miserable body. Now, can I get back to why I'm here right now?"

"Sure."

"When Senator Melon exposed you in an effort to weaken the President, that left you in a vacuum. Nothing lasts very long in that state. Also, I have fallen out of favor with Hoover. Thus, it is finally time to combine our talents on a mission that neither one of us has been able to solve on our own."

"You seem to be doing quite well without me," Meeker argued. "After all, you've been to his headquarters and know his name. I bring very little to the table."

"I was there yesterday," Bryant admitted, "but he was gone. But don't sell yourself short. You know a great deal more than you realize. And, in truth, neither of us can do this on our own. So, are you ready to show the world what two powerful women can do?"

Helen Meeker wasn't ready to answer.

ABOUT THE AUTHOR

Ace Collins is the writer of more than sixty books, including several bestsellers: *Stories behind the Best-Loved Songs of Christmas*, *Stories behind the Great Traditions of Christmas*, *The Cathedrals*, and *Lassie: A Dog's Life*. Based in Arkadelphia, Arkansas, He continues to publish several new titles each year, including a series of novels, the first of which is *Farraday Road*. Ace has appeared on scores of television shows, including CBS This Morning, NBC Nightly News, CNN, Good Morning America, MSNBC, and Entertainment Tonight.

Made in the USA
Charleston, SC
17 September 2016